THE MOVIE STAR

21st Century Courtesan: Book Two

P. S. DUMOND
PAMELA DUMOND

Pamela DuMond Media

Ebook ISBN-13: 978-1-941731-07-9
Print ISBN-978-1-941731-07-9

Photo: Adobe Stock
Cover by Glammypammy

Published by Pamela DuMond Media

ALSO BY PAMELA DUMOND

THRILLERS

21st CENTURY COURTESAN series

THE PLAYER #1
THE MOVIE STAR #2
THE BELOVED #3
THE HUSBAND #4
THE DEVOTED FAN #5

MORTAL BELOVED TIME TRAVEL series

The Messenger #1
The Assassin #2
The Seeker #3
The Believer #4: Jack & Clara — STAND ALONE

COZY MYSTERIES

ANNIE GRACELAND COZY MYSTERIES Stand Alones

Cupcakes, Pies, & Hometown Guys
Cupcakes, Sales, & Cocktails
Cupcakes, Diaries, & Rotten Inquiries
Cupcakes, Paws, & Bad Santa Claus
Cupcakes, Bats, & Scaredy Cats
Cupcakes, Bars, & Rock Stars
Cupcakes, Spies, & Despicable Guys
Cupcakes, Lies, & Dead Guys

VON PUMPERNICKLE COZY MYSTERIES

Goldmitten

'SWEETER' ROMANCE

ROYALLY WED ROM-COM series

Part-time Princess #1
Royally Wed #2
Part-time Poser #3
Royally Knocked Up #4

PLAYING SWEETER ROM-COM Stand Alones

Ms. Match Meets a Millionaire
The Story of You and Me

'HOT' ROMANCE

THE CROWN AFFAIR series

The Prince's Playbook #1
His Majesty's Measure #2
The American Princess #3
The Duchess's Decision #4

PLAYING DIRTY ROM-COM Stand Alones

The Client
The Matchmaker
The Bodyguard

THE MOVIE STAR: Book Two

Gorgeous movie star Jake Keller's on track to win an Oscar. But Jake's shutting down, going off grid, doing nothing to help promote his chances.

Evie travels to Hollywood to try and help discover what -- or who -- broke Jake. But dirty little secrets prefer to stay buried...

—

I'm a 21ST CENTURY COURTESAN.

Beautiful, broken men pay Ma Maison Agency ungodly sums of money to be with me because I'm empathic: I feel their emotions in my body. I track down the bitter belief that broke them and then I help them heal.

I'm down to my last four clients. One wants to play me. One wants to buy me. **One wants to marry me. And one wants to murder me. *Will I get out in time...***

PRAISE for 21ST CENTURY COURTESAN

"**...breath-taking, beautiful, and brilliant.** A must-read..." *USA Today* bestselling author Maggie Marr

"**I am ADDICTED!** If I could give this book more than

five stars I would. I devoured it in less than 4 hours... I can't wait for the next installment." Liz Vrchota

"...original, suspenseful, mysterious, sexy, and dramatic... a captivating read." Angela Hayes

"...was completely enthralled and **blown away by this book!"** Vegas Daisy

For the Survivors

Because the wounds aren't always visible.

"I have decided to stick with love. Hate is too great a burden to bear."

Martin Luther King, Jr.

❧ I ❧

BEFORE

BEFORE

BLOOD PUMPS THROUGH MY ARTERIES, MY MUSCLES GEAR UP
to throw punches and dodge bullets while my brain tries to
figure out if there's really a problem. My body knows when
someone wants to hurt me. It's had a lot of practice.

One Saturday afternoon in the 6th grade I hung out at my
friend Emily's house. The music was loud. Her sister was
hosting a pizza party after a high school football game. A guy
with bloodshot eyes stared at me from the far end of the
kitchen, his hand caressing the watery drops beading on his
soft drink can. Just looking at him made my stomach lurch
about like the pizza I'd eaten was bad.

I didn't want to get sick at Emily's house, so I went
upstairs and grabbed my coat from her bed. When I turned
to leave the guy with the bloodshot eyes was standing in the
doorway breathing heavily and staring at me funny. I
slammed the door in his face. I jammed the lock and sat on

the bed, my heart rattling about in my chest like a ghost haunting a closet.

He knocked and knocked. I squeezed my eyes shut and hugged my arms around my ribs because I knew no one would hear me over the music if I hollered for help.

When the music finally quieted, I popped open the door and peered into the hallway: he was gone. I bolted down the stairs and didn't stop running until I got home. A few months later that guy's face was plastered across our local paper because he had hurt a different girl at a different party.

"It's him, Mom," I said.

"See what I told you about respecting your instincts?" Mom made stir fry, the frozen vegetables simmered in the pan. "I bet that girl didn't do the smart girl thing."

"But what if she did?" I asked. "What if that girl fought back and hollered but no one heard her scream over the music?" My stomach knows when a situation is dangerous.

My bones know when someone dies. I was seven when Grandma Berlinger popped up in my dream shaking her owl-head baking spoon at me, fussing that she was taking a trip. "I'm out of here, munchkin," she said. "I'm putting you in charge of taking care of your Mom."

I woke with a start, the covers still tucked around me and yet there was a coldness in my bones, a heaviness that hadn't been there when I'd nodded off. Sure enough, Mom got the phone call the next morning that Grandma Berlinger had passed away in the middle of the night.

Now it's been seven long, heartbreaking days since we ran into the Wolfe brothers. A week since they bounced off our car, flew through the air like broken birds, and no one will tell me if they're alive or dead.

No one will answer my questions. No one will take me seriously because I'm just that poor girl whose mother had a psychotic split. I'm that 'sorry child' who crawled out of the car toward the brothers bleeding on the cold, hard, white snow. I'm the– 'Shh, don't say that loud enough for Evelyn Berlinger to hear' that her mother is going to jail for this you know' girl.

I bet rumors are circulating about the Wolfe boys back at Beethoven Middle Grade school, but I'm not there to hear them. Mom's been taken away, Ruby and I have been split up and sent to different foster homes. I'm staying in a different town with a perfectly nice woman in a house with other sad kids. But in spite of everything I know in my bones that Wyatt Wolfe is not dead.

If only I had Bones on speed dial. I'd pay my entire monthly allowance to hear him pick up. 'How may we help you?' Bones would ask.

'Just calling to find out if Wyatt Wolfe's still alive?' I'd pinch myself as a reminder to keep breathing, not hold my breath and pass out because I'm so dizzy from the anxiety wriggling under my skin.

'He's not only alive, Evie, but he's doing great,' Bones would say. 'A few of us were broken in the accident but we're all healing up now. Thanks for asking.'

'Oh, good,' I'd say, relief coursing through me like a sugary soda. 'I've been wondering 'cause he and his brother Easton haven't been back to school. And I need to tell them how incredibly sorry I am. I need them to forgive me."

'Give it time.' Bones would say. "Forgiveness can take some time.'

I PRAY FOR FORGIVENESS EVERY NIGHT.

But now a month or so has passed since the accident and I don't see the Wolfe boys, and there is no chance to say I'm sorry. There's no forgiveness for Mom either because she's being sentenced to six months in jail today and my heart twists like laundry fresh out of the drier threatening to choke me.

After the hearing, a woman escorts me down a maze of hallways into a room where I get to see Mom before they take her off to wherever she'll serve her sentence. "Evie," Mom says, her arms out wide.

"Oh, Mom." I run into her arms, swallowing tears. I press my head against her chest and shudder. She hugs me tight.

She pulls back and tucks a lock of hair behind my ear. "It's going to be okay," she says. "I did something stupid. I did something bad. This is the best way for me to pay for my sins. I'm not going to be gone that long and you're going to be okay. You always are."

"I don't know." I worry my lower lip.

"You're going to be just fine because you're my oldest child. You're my rock." She grips my forearm. It cuts like a knife. "You'll be the strong sister for Ruby."

"Ruby's not living with me, Mom."

"I know. You're still my oldest girl. Promise me you'll be strong for Ruby."

"I don't know."

"Come on. We'll pray on it." She crosses herself, then grabs my hand so hard. "Dear Jesus. Please help Evie stay strong while I'm in jail."

"Dear Jesus. Please help me stay strong while Mom's in jail."

Mom squeezes her eyes shut. "Dear God, help Evie stay strong so I can heal and pay my debt."

Mom's feelings boomerang inside me. I have to hold it together for her. "Please help me stay strong so Mom can heal and pay her debt."

"Help Evie stay strong so Ruby can grow up healthy," she prays.

I feel so small. I bow my head and repeat, "Please help me stay strong so Ruby can grow up healthy."

"And this I ask for in the name of the Father and the Son and the Holy Spirit," Mom says. "Amen."

"And this I ask for in the name of the Father and the Son and the Holy Spirit. Amen."

"You're my good girl, Evelyn." She opens her eyes, releases my hand, and kisses my cheek. "I love you. I'll be back home with you and Ruby in no time."

"Okay." I wiggle my fingers to get the blood back into them as the woman leads her away.

Mom stops at the door and stares at me wistfully. "Count on it, Evie."

"I'm counting on it, Mom."

FRACTURED FANTASIES

FRACTURED FANTASIES

———

THE FIRST TIME I SAW JAKE KELLER, MOVIE STAR, I WAS thirteen-years-old. It was before the accident when we still lived with Mom's boyfriend, Kyle Monroe.

Mom took Ruby and me to one of Jake's movies on the spur of the moment. I shoved popcorn in my mouth and watched him on the big screen, mesmerized.

Jake's blonde hair. The determined look on his face when he stared down at that girl as the rain pelted them. But most of all, it was his eyes. Kind and gentle and sexy. It was all I could do not to yell at the screen, 'Kiss that girl who is staring up at you in the rain. Please kiss her now before I explode!'

"He needs to kiss her," Mom said.

Ruby leaned over me and tapped Mom on her knee. "Can I go to the bathroom?"

"You just went," Mom said.

And when Jake finally put his hands on that girl's face,

when he finally pulled her to him and gazed into her eyes. When he finally kissed her -- Mom and I both sighed, looked at each other, and burst out giggling.

Ruby jiggled her foot on the floor. "Can I go *now?*"

"Yes," Mom said.

Jake Keller is *that* kind of actor. His characters transcend time and space, make all the hair on the back of your neck stand up like soldiers on parade. Now he's one of the biggest movie stars in the world. Maybe it's nostalgia that makes me want to find out what damaged him. Maybe it's a need to return to a more innocent time, before the accident, that makes me want to save him. I certainly wouldn't be the first fool to be motivated by nostalgia.

I'm flying from Chicago to L.A. tomorrow to help Jake Keller heal. I'll wear expensive, designer clothes. I'll accompany him to celebrity parties. We'll be photographed sharing intimate dinners at elegant restaurants and impossibly trendy cafes. Undoubtedly, I'll show up in a handful of gossip sites as 'Jake Keller Out and About with 'Unnamed Twenty-something Brunette.'

Healing a damaged movie star might look shiny and glamorous but trust me it's not. I'll keep long hours and get spotty sleep. I'll dig into his psyche, find his dirty secrets, willingly sacrifice my grip on sanity. I'll do it to track down the core belief that's murdering his mojo. I'll do it to help him heal and in the process I'll make a fortune.

Healing broken men is filthy, grueling work, which is why it's ironic that on the outside I look immaculate. I look fucking flawless. My body's toned from hours of working out. My hair is glossy. My skin glows from the sugar scrub that makes it baby soft to a man's touch. I'm a shiny fucking penny.

But scratch the surface and you'll sink through my very thin skin and light on the jangled, tangled mess of my nerves because some predator invaded my home tonight and left a jewelry box filled with a Bible verse and locks of cut hair on my bed.

Instead of hitting the sack early and getting a good night's sleep before I fly to L.A., I huddle outside my red brick, 12-story condo building and chew on what several hours ago was a perfectly manicured fingernail. My 70-something neighbor, Hazel O'Rourke and her scrappy dog, Ruca keep me company.

"You're young, pretty, and good hearted," Hazel says. "You're bound to attract your fair share of jealous friends as well as creeps. Trust me, I've seen my share of weirdos but this one takes the cake. The cops are finally here, thank God."

The police SUV parks right under the "No Parking" sign. Ruca, eight pounds of fierceness, yips up a soprano aria, as the uniformed cops make their way toward us.

"Do you want me to stay?" Hazel asks.

"Nah, I'm cool. Thanks for waiting with me as long as you did."

"No problem." She plucks Ruca off the ground. "If you need anything, just knock."

"Will do." I salute her. I answer the officers' questions. Yes, I've received a handful of weird letters in the past, but it's been about a year since the last one. No, I don't have a clue who would want to do something like this. My work? I'm a 'consultant for high end corporations'.

This kind of intrusion isn't normal in my profession. Does anyone have a key to my place? Hmm. Not since I moved six months ago. Fresh locks. Fresh keys.

"I'll walk you inside," I say.

"Best if we check out your place first," one of the cops says.

I hand him my keychain. "Unit 1211."

"It's normal to feel scared," says Detective Novak the female officer who stays behind with me. "It's a violation. Do you have anyone you can call, Ms. Berlinger? Family? A friend?"

"Yes," I say, then think about it. "But they're probably working."

"Night shift's a bitch," she says. "Stay here. One of us will be back in no time." She walks inside, the door swinging shut behind her, leaving me all alone on a humid, big city evening under a hazy night sky. I pull out my phone and swipe the pictures I took of the letter the intruder left. And I read:

Dear Evelyn:

It's been two years. I had hoped by now you would have grown your hair back. But there is no covering, there is no modest Evelyn, there is only boastful Evelyn. Proud Evelyn. Evelyn who flaunts everything she has.

And this disturbs me.

I'm not sure what to do about this. I'm weighing options. I'm just a mess inside and yet you sleep easily. Some days I can't eat and worry gnaws at my bones.

And I wonder — what if Evelyn doesn't have a covering and some kind of sicko realizes that and picks a fight with her? Evelyn used to be awfully nice, but she's changed. She shows off. She's entitled. Now she's putting herself out there. Right there in the crosshairs for just the right predator to come around and take,

take, take whatever they want from Evelyn. Whatever they crave.

What do you think they'll take first, Evelyn? Your covering's gone. I'm disappointed in you. So very disappointed. I've been silent a while, but I can be silent no more. I just had to say something. I hope you don't mind.

I only want your best, Evelyn.

I am, as always,

Your Devoted Fan

I shiver, shove my phone back in my purse, and slide down the brick wall until my ass hits the pavement. I stare east at the lights twinkling off the skyscrapers in Chicago's downtown business district. By day the Loop is the working capital of the Midwest, chock full of lawyers, bankers, and money makers. I probably make more than eighty percent of those folks.

I'm twenty-six years old and recently cracked seven figures a year. I didn't invent a miracle drug that cures cancer. I didn't configure a social media platform that went viral. I wouldn't know how to build a hot money making app if it flew through the air and punched me in the eye. I earn big money because I'm a 21st Century Courtesan. Beautiful, broken, wealthy men hire me to help them heal.

I'm empathic. I feel what they're feeling in my body. Their core wounds twist through me and I identify the emotions behind them. What is rooting about in my belly?

His shame. What's the sensation compressing my chest? His heartache.

The men I help are titans of their industries. When I serve up their fucked up belief — the thing that's shutting them down – all neat and pretty tied with a bow on a platter – I offer them deliverance. I grant them absolution. Once they've got the keys to their kingdom in hand, they don't need me anymore. And with the exception of Dylan McAlister, the first client I helped over a year ago – I never hear from them again.

But right now, I'm not feeling all Glinda the good witch sparkly waving her wand about, dispensing magical ruby slippers. Right now, I'm just a scared twenty something girl huddling alone next to her building wearing leggings and a "Will Give Medical Advice for Tacos" T-shirt at night in a big city neighborhood. I desperately need family but that fantasy fractured a long time ago. I break down and text Amelia.

Evie: You around?

Amelia: Working. Can't talk right now.

Amelia: You OK?

Evie: Yeah. Something weird.

Amelia: Nothing with Movie Star, right? The L.A. gig's still on.

Evie: Nothing with Movie Star.

Evie: No worries. Talk later.

Amelia: K.

Amelia: *Text me if you need anything.*

I stand back up and pace a few yards in front of the building, practically carving a trench in the sidewalk. I'm not going to call Dylan my part-time boyfriend. I haven't seen him in a few months. Over a year ago he thought that if I cut off all my hair I'd be safer. Better able to ward off whatever stalker problems I might have had. As much as I love this man, God, he can worry with the best of them.

I can't call my mom. She's pissed off at me, huddled in her suite at the mental health Institute binge streaming shows because I canceled our vacation to the lake house. I also can't call Ruby. She left Meth Head boyfriend, graduated to Married Man boyfriend, and is still tragically useless in the support department. I'll be damned if I'm calling Madame Marchand unless my hair catches on fire and there's no water available in a mile wide radius.

But I really don't want to be alone. I text Victoria.

Evie: *Hey. Good time to talk?*

Victoria*: Perfect. What's up?*

I text back so fast my thumbs are tripping over each other. I fill her in that someone broke into my place and left a jewelry box filled with hair on my bed.

Victoria*: Wait a minute. What? Holy shit on a shingle!*

Victoria: *Someone left a jewelry box with hair on your bed?*

Victoria*: That's wacked.*

Victoria: *On my way.*

Evie: *Don't --*

Evie: *Seriously, the cops are already here.*

Victoria*: Good. I would have called them if you hadn't. See you in 10.*

She's here in five. We sit cross legged on the sidewalk. "Who do you think would do this?" she asks.

I shrug. "I don't know but didn't something like this happen to you?"

"Yes," she says, lighting matches and blowing them out. "Did the weirdo leave a letter?"

"Yes." I hold out my phone to her.

She swipes through the photos and shudders. "Jesus. This isn't about me, but it brings back crappy memories. I'm so sorry you're going through this."

The cops return 45 minutes later.

"Ms. Berlinger," Detective Novak says. "Nothing's missing? Is that correct?"

"Right."

"Plenty of times folks discover things missing later. Don't hesitate to call me." She hands me her card. "We're taking the box to the lab and going to run it for prints. The lab will analyze the hair but I'm pretty sure it's synthetic. I've known my share of weaves and wigs."

"Me too," Victoria pipes up.

"Feel free to call us or we'll get ahold of you," she says, steps back in their SUV and they drive away.

My home has been broken into and I've been violated. Dylan was right and wrong all at the same time: a predator *does* have me in his sights and it *does* have something to do with my hair. It's just not playing out exactly how he imagined. Violation and its first cousin, disgust, slither across me and I'm suddenly overwhelmed by the need to shower with an entire bottle of disinfectant.

I look up at my corner condo on the top floor. How in the hell did this creep get in? Maybe he went over the roof, took the fire escape down and shimmied over the ledge. I did it once when I was locked out. Scary, but not impossible. I'm going to have to call a locksmith and put extra security on the windows but I can't do that tonight.

My safety bubble has been slashed, air hissing out of formerly cushy tires. The keys, resting cool in my hand feel unfamiliar and that pisses me off. I've worked so hard to get to a place of balance, juggling my crazy mom, sister with the bad boyfriend picker, demanding job, and broken men. This feels like the last straw right at a time when I need to be strong because the biggest job of my life starts tomorrow. I clench the keys so hard the grooves dig into my skin and I don't know whether to cry or scream.

"You want to stay at my place tonight?" Victoria asks.

"Yes," I say. "Yes, I do."

🥮 3 🥮

BRIGHT LIGHTS

BRIGHT LIGHTS

I PITCH SOME MAKEUP, SHOES, CLOTHES, AND JEWELRY IN two suitcases, finally roll out of my place at 1 a.m. and crash for the rest of this lost night at Victoria's place. We're both wound tighter than a couple of two dollar watches so we stay up and talk until 3 a.m.

"Can you tell me about what happened with your stalker thing?" I ask

"Maybe tonight's not the best night to share that."

"You're right," I say. "Thank you for everything."

"We're cool, Kindergarten," she says, calling me by my nickname. "Don't let what happened tonight screw up getting your new job done. It's a big one. I'm rooting for you."

"That's super nice of you. Why are you rooting for me?"

"You know. The changeover at Ma Maison management."

"There's a changeover at Ma Maison management?"

"That's the rumor. No one's guaranteed a job after the

shakeup. Only the strong survive. Get some sleep while you can. Oh, and call me if you need anything while you're in L.A. I've got friends there." She shuffles down the hallway in her pajamas with cartoon cats jumping around on them.

I catch a few hours of fitful sleep and pat on extra under eye concealer the next morning before heading out to Midway Airport. It looks like it might rain. Thick clouds bump across the sky.

I wash my hands, stare into the tinny mirror in the airport bathroom when fear bubbles up in my stomach like bad chili mac and cheese. I start to panic. What if we hit turbulence? Oh super, this flight is going to be bumpy as shit.

'Wait a second.' Hope, my internal optimist reasons. *'You're not scared of flying. You're picking up on someone else's anxiety. You're getting an empathic hit.'*

'Right.' I concentrate and pinch the acupressure spot on the thick web of flesh between my thumb and forefinger, the sharp sensation grounding me.

'You're tired,' Hope says. *'Find the person you're picking up on.'*

I don't have far to look. The anxiety belongs to the woman standing at the sink next to me. She's middle-aged, rubbing her hands over and over under the water, her fingers red, practically raw. My gut twists, confirming that she's terrified to fly. It's her fear that bubbles up inside me.

'Not yours,' Queasy says. *'Handle it.'*

I count *three, two, one* and sink into my meditative level. The internal space that lies between conscious and subconscious. The place that nurtures dreams and hopes and intention.

I can see this woman's fear in my mind's eye: it's a small, dense, gray cloud. It's been nagging her for a while, making her worry about money and relationships and what happens if the plane she's in falls from the sky.

Who will feed her fish if she's dead?

Will anyone find her last will and testament? It's in the second drawer down on the left side of her desk.

I tell her fear to shut up for a second and I visualize pushing that cloud out of me and releasing it back to the universe where it can be repurposed into positive energy. Ten seconds later that negative ball is gone. I toss a quick prayer to the heavens that God, or the Universe, helps this woman calm down before the plane takes off, or at very least the flight attendant comps her a stiff cocktail. Maybe I'll buy her one.

I head to my gate and grab an overdue coffee at a kiosk. Out of nowhere exhaustion slides like thick mud down the back of my skull and my neck until it hits the base of my spine. I move from wired to dog-tired in ten seconds and suddenly the floor looks awfully comfy.

I might be running on empty, but unless I just got infected with Mono, I'm not *this* tired. Ugh. *Another* empathic hit. Another uncomfortable feeling that's not mine. Apparently being violated has opened the floodgates to all sorts of crappy sensations to tromp about, picking at me like opportunistic thieves.

My gaze is drawn to a seventy-something guy in a rumpled suit running a veiny hand through thinning hair. He's staring at his laptop screen. There are dark circles under his eyes. This mudslide is *his* exhaustion. Oh man, someone needs to slap some sense into me because I need to get a handle on these uninvited empathic hits *now*.

I don't have the emotional bandwidth to handle every uncomfortable sensation slopping around me like dirty mop water. I need to bring my A game to Hollywood to handle Jake Keller's needs. *Get a grip, Evie. Get a fucking grip.* I board the plane as soon as the attendant announces First Class boarding. I sit back in my seat, close my eyes, and visualize erecting an emotional wall within me – brick by brick. I will myself to keep others' uninvited, debilitating feelings out.

I'm perfunctorily nice to the guy next to me. He's an accountant at a big 10 firm, super sweet, with no ring on the significant finger. He hands me his card with a glint of hope and attraction in his eyes and I'm tempted for a long moment.

Wouldn't this be a nice life? Married to Mr. Normal. Bearing normal children. Sunday dinners around a normal dining room table. Ballet and soccer and hockey and theatre for our delightfully normal kids. If only. Besides, Dylan McAlister's been threatening to put a ring on my finger for eighteen months but I'll believe it when I see it.

I slip the card inside my wallet, thank him, then turn away and take most of the flight to nap, meditate, and rebuild my emotional reserves. I slip on earphones, listen to guided meditations, ColdPlay, and Bach. Four and a half hours later the plane's landing gear rumbles, and the Captain announces our descent into L.A. I cross my fingers praying that I've got my shit together.

Dear God:

It's me, Evie. Checking in. Don't want to bug you. Don't want to take too much time from all the more important things you've got going on. Children in cages. Journalists getting murdered. But I'm a little shaky from last night. Please help me do my best for this man. Please help me track down what broke him so he can heal. Thank you. In the name of the Father, and the Son, and the Holy Spirit. Amen.

At Baggage Claim a female chauffeur swings a sign with my name above her head. She could be one of those twirlers on a street corner advertising a new strip mall. I'm grateful she swings that sign high and wide because in the capital of big money, bigger stars, and massive egos, I might not have seen her in the crush she is so tiny. I signal her with a wave.

"Ms. Berlinger?"

"Yes." I walk toward her.

"Awesome! How was your flight?"

"Uneventful," I say. "Thanks for asking."

"That's the best kind," she says. "My name's Nikki. Follow me." She wears a fitted black pant suit and is about five years younger than me. She reminds me of my sister Ruby before she hooked up with Meth Head Boyfriend. Sweet. Earnest.

"I'll grab your suitcases," she says.

"Nope. I'll handle that."

"Let me," she says. "The security guys tease me that I can't keep up with them."

"How long has that bullshit been going on?"

"Since I started the job a few months ago," she says. "Don't worry. It's kind of like pledging to be a Little Sister at a frat house."

"What if pledging lasts longer than a few months?"

"Then I'll have to beat one of the assholes at pool, poker, or darts."

She's smart. I like her. "If that doesn't work?"

"I'll resort to my fierce uppercut," She flexes her thin arm and grins, so much like my sister, it etches a tiny crack in my heart. "Or I'll pitch a dart at their head."

I smile. "The two black bags with the raspberry stripes coming down the chute are mine."

"On it," she says.

Forty minutes later I'm sitting in the back of a town car checking messages as Nikki drives up L.A.'s Sunset Strip past the pop and glow of trendy shops and restaurants. I put my phone down and take in the magic of the City of Angels. There's a store for just about anything and everything in L.A. Ceramics. Clothing. Electronics. Dating App Headquarters.

"Traffic's not as bad as I expected," I say.

"It's a weekday and there's no A list special events." Nikki makes a quick left onto a residential street. "Traffic's a freaking nightmare during weekends, spring break, and award season."

"Which leaves what kind of window?".

"Tonight."

I laugh. The car's engine purrs as we climb a hill passing houses anchored on stilts deep into steep mountainsides. "It's gorgeous," I say, my gaze alternating between the imposing mansions and the twinkling lights of the Sunset Strip below.

"If you like your dose of beautiful with bling, bright lights and hoopla."

"On occasion, I do." I wonder if the people on the Strip need to take a break. Go to their own version of a Wisconsin lake house, dip their toes in gunky green lake water. Reboot. That's what I should be doing right now. Taking a vacation at a little cabin at the end of a dirt lane surrounded by woods, backed up onto a lake. I'm lucky that the lodge's proprietor kept my down payment, and graciously bumped the date because they were able to fill the slot. If only Mom was that forgiving.

I'm bummed I have to delay my vacation but I don't regret it. I open my bag and pull out the packet on Jake Keller. There is something about his picture that calls to me. Something haunted in his face, his eyes that makes me want to be his guardian. His warrior princess. I already wonder about his core wound. What shut him down.

Movie Star Jake Keller is the reason I am here in L.A. He's thirty-seven years old, a successful A list actor, banked ten million on his last starring role. He's starring in a new movie and getting early Oscar buzz. But he's shut down. He's not taking meetings. He's not campaigning for the award that could cement his career. His support team is freaking out.

I flip through a few of his photos. He's ridiculously handsome in that doesn't- work-too-hard-for-it way. A slow burn simmers in his brown eyes and a grin plays at the corner of his upper lip. His body is hot. Ripped shoulders. Defined muscles. Narrow waist. Washboard abs. Tight ass.

'Oh, come on, Evie,' my negative voice, Queasy says, rolling over in my stomach with a disturbing thunk that makes me wince. *'Pictures of actors are photo-shopped. No one's that ridiculously hot.'*

He *is* that hot, I silently insist.

'In your dreams,' Queasy says.

"Any questions I can answer before we get to Jake's place?" Nikki asks.

"If you're offering I'm not about to say no." I rifle through more documents. "What did they tell you about me?"

"Pinkie Stein said you're some kind of consultant brought in to help Jake with his anxiety."

"That sounds about right," I say. "Pinkie was quoted in a tabloid as saying he wasn't attending events because he was 'floating.' What does she mean by that?"

"She's his PR person," Nikki says. "She distracts. She's an expert at smoke and mirrors."

"Got it," I say. In the picture clipped to her page on the document she sports shimmery champagne blonde hair with pink, blue, and green highlights, plump collagen enhanced lips, and a heart as big as Kansas sunshine. She looks about ten years older than Jake. "Do you like Pinkie?"

"Who doesn't?" Nikki says. "She was with Jake before he hit the big leagues. She'll probably be with him in forty years after he disappears from it."

"A weird question." I say. If Nikki's honest with me it'll save me time and I'll feel it in my gut.

"Shoot."

"Friend or foe?"

"Friend."

Queasy's silent for a change meaning her answer rings true

in my gut. I've got a friend in Nikki and probably one in Pinkie Stein. "Pinkie's in love with Jake, right?"

"Def," Nikki says. "But she has no illusions. No problems 'sharing' her imaginary 'husband' with you if she likes you. Just don't get drunk with her at a party. You'll hop a red-eye on a dare and end up in Cabo sipping Bloody Mary's lying next to an infinity pool overlooking the ocean while muscular men massage you."

"Heaven. What about Adam Bachman?"

"Jake's producing partner?"

"Yup."

"High strung." Nikki turns the car left onto a side street, the engine kicking into a different gear as we climb a steeper road.

I've already researched Adam Bachman and so far, Nikki's two for two.

"Drama follows Adam around like baby flies nursing on a tit of shit," she says.

"The polar opposite of Pinkie."

"Understatement," Nikki says, her voice rising to a falsetto. "'Jake! *Hollywood Reporter* called! Jake! *Vanity Fair* wants an interview and a photoshoot. Jacob! Why are you doing this to me?'"

I stifle giggles. "Are you an actress?"

"Kind of. Well, I used to be, but not anymore."

"You didn't like it?"

"Loved it. Just wasn't in the cards."

"You'd be surprised what's in the cards," I say.

"The cards are over-rated."

'The kid's sweet, but she's not your client.' Queasy rumbles. *'Pick your battles.'*

"What about Jake's agent, Ray Stark?"

"Mr. I Don't Give A Fuck, Make it Happen Ray Stark?"

"Yup."

"I'm one of the little people," she says. "I don't even blip on Ray Stark's radar."

The Santa Monica mountains stretch in front of us as she turns another corner. We wind up a thinner lane filled with short driveways ending in large, but discrete garages, the houses built behind them perched on canyon hills on stilts that anchor them into the bedrock. My ears pop.

Nikki three point turns the black Jeep and parks adjacent to a Spanish styled house, its driveway already filled with a collection of Ferraris, Porsches and a few clunkers. Benzes and Land Rovers line the street. "Home sweet, home," she says opening my door.

"In the future? You don't need to wait on me." I slip her a hundred.

"Oh, but I do," she says. "The one time I didn't I never heard the end of it."

"Jake gave you a rough time?" I love helping troubled souls. I'm not all that keen, however, on spending a month max, let alone a night, with a dick. "Is Jake Keller an asshole to you?"

"Good God, no." Nikki pops the trunk and pulls out my bags. "He's a great guy. Total yumsicle." She carts my bags to a door within the garage. She punches in a code into a keypad and a lock clicks open.

"Okay." I follow her into the tidy three car garage, two motorcycles, a couple of dirt bikes, and a golf cart parked on the far end. Muffled pop music throbs through the walls. "Jake golfs?"

"I think he does it to please his friends," she says, leading me to a door. Hot dance tunes hit us, blasting from a high-end sound system. Camillo Cabello wails from the loud-speakers as we enter through the laundry room and suddenly find ourselves in the middle of a party.

Nikki's wheeling both my bags, navigating around stacked

cases of water and beer. One of my bags smacks into a laundry basket on the floor and she struggles to yank it free.

"Let me help," I say and take one from her. We make our way into the kitchen It's suddenly noisier and a lot more crowded because we're smack dab in the middle of a party.

"Hey," a man says. "I'll carry those."

"Thanks," I say. "But we've got this."

"It's my house," he says. "At the end of the day I decide who carries what in my house."

I turn and see the reason why I am here.

Jake Keller.

❦ 4 ❦

MAGIC TOUCH

MAGIC TOUCH

I'VE BEEN IN THE ROOM WITH MY FAIR SHARE OF POWERFUL, dynamic tycoons. But star power sizzles off Jake Keller like sparklers on the 4th of July and suddenly the floor feels a little shaky under my feet. "That's awfully nice of you."

"That's awfully bossy of you," Nikki says.

"That's awfully *normal* of me," Jake says.

"Since when have you been normal, dork?" Nikki asks.

"Since always, dorkette."

If these two aren't siblings they should be.

I search for sensations, clues, empathic reactions to my latest client, but my stomach is not clenching in guilt, my heart not racing in fear. Except for the excitement from the pretty sparklers I'm getting nothing and it throws me.

Is there something wrong with me? Am I damaged from last night's violation?

'Don't go down the 'There must be something wrong with Me' road,' Hope says.

'You just got here. Shake this shit off,' Queasy says. *'Focus on something positive.'*

I center myself because Hope and Queasy are right. I focus on the positive, which is right in front of me. Jake's just as handsome in person as he is in his pictures. He sports dimples a girl longs to run a finger over. His slow burn eyes linger with curiosity on my face. His lips quirk into his signature million dollar smile but this time that smile's directed at me. God help me, *now* my body's reacting like a teenager's.

"You must be Evelyn," he says.

"I am." I extend my hand. His grip is firm, his palm warm. "Call me Evie."

"Jake Keller. Good to meet you. Thanks for traveling from Chicago." He commandeers my bags. "Follow me."

"Sure thing," I say and can't help but notice how his jeans fit his ass – all snug and deliriously happy to be close to him.

Nikki shoves back a grin. "Busted!"

"Sorry!" I say. "I've always wondered – real? Or photoshopped?"

"He works out a lot." She whispers behind a raised hand as Jake makes his way through the kitchen, skirting around the beautiful people who pretend that they are minding their own business when it's pretty obvious that the only business they are minding is Jake's. "I bet that's all his. No ass implants."

"Stop talking about my ass with everyone you meet, Nikki," he says without turning around. "You're going to give Evie the wrong impression. You're off the clock."

She frowns. "Oh, come on –"

"I mean it. Go. Brandt keeps asking about you. Something about a 'friendly' game of pool. He's telling the guys that he's going to kick your itty-bitty girl ass."

"Brandt likes to brag," she says. "Bragging makes up for his itty-bitty boy dick."

I cough and slap a hand over my mouth.

"Ha," Jake says. "Be gone, Nikki."

"If you need anything, text," Nikki says to me. "I not only work for Casa Keller, I hang here too."

"Will do," I say. "Thanks."

Jake beckons me to follow him. "Tell me about your trip."

"Uneventful," I say.

"Don't you love when that happens?"

"I do."

We make our way through the kitchen past a gaggle of scantily-attired, overly made up women probably my age, even though they act a million years younger. They pose, smile, and take selfies next to a built in shelf loaded with gilded statues, plaques, and awards.

"You probably already know how this works," he says.

I have no idea what he's talking about. "Why don't you explain it to me?" I follow him through a hallway, past a large family room filled with leather furniture, a billiards table, a few TVs high on the walls, and a carved wooden bar in the corner next to a jukebox.

"There's a party going on tonight. Nothing big. Nothing fancy. I'm pulling suitcases with raspberry stripes on the top. Definitely not my luggage. You're pretty, a new face at Casa Keller and that makes you mysterious. I'll guarantee you rumors are already spreading faster than a video of a fat cat grooming a litter of baby raccoons."

"Got it," I say.

"People will ask you questions that seem innocent but they're about as harmless as Odysseus gifting the Trojan horse."

"I should be careful?"

"Yup."

His eyes are soft. Curious. They hold a certain sweetness.

"One more thing," he says.

"Yes?" I stare up into his eyes. The same eyes that looked down at that girl in the rain on the big screen before he kissed her, and for a few heartbeats I totally get how she must have felt. Wanted. Needed. Special.

"My ass is one hundred percent real."

I bust out laughing, and snort before I recover. "Good to know."

He grins back at me. "Come on." He leads me through back corridors, passing people tossing back shots, laughing, nibbling from small plates of food, and schmoozing.

"Don't you need to hang out with them?" I ask.

"Nope." He leads me past a living room with vaulted ceilings and a brilliant chandelier.

"Hey Jake," a familiar looking metro guy calls out from across the room. "Someone here I want you to meet."

"In a bit Adam," he hollers over the music. "You're my perfect excuse to not be with them. I'm busy because I have a VIP in from out of town."

"That's sweet." My cheeks grow warm. "Please don't stop yourself from work or play because of me."

"If you weren't here I'd be in hiding."

"Do you always hide during parties?"

"For the most part – yes. I don't throw the parties. Adam, or one of the guys throws them. It's a never-ending arsenal of ideas to cheer me up."

He walks in the direction of a gaggle of pretty girls in a mirrored hallway who frantically preen while pretending to ignore him. "You and I never talked before my agent hired you."

"Is that awkward for you?"

"Not really," he says.

Out of nowhere it feels like a knife rips into my stomach.

I trip over my own feet, catch myself, and recover all in a breath, but Jake notices.

"Tired?"

"A little," I say. I identify the sensation. Jealousy's stabbing me and it's coming from the cluster of girls we're approaching. I try to ignore the sensations. A petite blond juts her hip, a curvy redhead thrusts out her boobs. They're too busy preening to give a rat's ass about me.

The stabbing envy's coming from the brunette in the black miniskirt who tosses her hair and glares at me like I kidnapped her puppy. If looks could kill I'd be laid out on the floor bleeding out right now.

'She's not a bad girl,' Hope says, *'Just thirsty. Say a prayer that she finds happiness.'*

'Will do.' The thirsty brunette doesn't know I'm only here for a few weeks. Hanging out with Jake is work for me.

'Perhaps Thirsty can inch her mini-skirt a little higher during the next party,' Queasy says. *'Maybe that'll grab Jake's attention. Get rid of her negativity.'*

I take a breath, push the brunette's petty viciousness out of my body, and lob it back in her direction. She slaps her neck like a mosquito bit her.

"Let's cover the basics," Jake says.

"Okay."

"How long are you staying for?"

"Mr. Stark retained my services for a month."

"You going to help me heal?"

"I'll do my best."

"They all say that."

"They?"

"The experts that Ray hires."

"I'm not your one and only?" I bat my eyelashes theatrically, curious about the others.

"Sadly, no Bambi. You might however be the cutest. You ever get retained for a month but then finish the job early?"

"All the time. You on a tight schedule?"

"I don't know what I'm on anymore. Everything got turned around about six months ago."

"What happened six months ago?"

He ignores my question. "What if the job goes longer?"

"Mr. Stark can contact Madame Marchand at Ma Maison."

"Did Nikki give you the house rules?"

"No," I say, hoping it's the basics. Shower daily. Get dressed. Eat. Sleep. Let him buy me something expensive and pretty. Show me off to his friends. Most likely sleep with him at some point in time to help him heal. Hey – he's Jake Keller. I'd be a fool to complain.

"You need anything, ask," Jake says.

"Got it."

"You want to go anywhere," Jake says. "Nikki or one of the guys will drive you."

"Got it. Did Mr. Stark tell you anything about me? Like what I do? How I do it?"

"Nope. Just said he was bringing in another specialist. I'm starting to feel like an alien on the dissection table behind the triple locked door at the secret government facility."

"Your house is warm. Comfy," I say. "Not exactly a secret government facility."

"You just got here. You've never been to the basement."

"Besides alien dissection, what kind of government things go down in your basement?"

"Meetings," he says and keeps walking.

"What kind of meetings?"

"The usual. Diplomacy. Foreign affairs. Who's coming to town. The Chinese, the Koreans. A man walks past carrying a paint bucket and a few brushes. He waves to Jake. "The painters," Jake adds. "Food's in the kitchen, Jose. Help yourself."

"Gracias, Señor Keller."

"De nada," he says.

"The Painters?" I ask

"Yup. Don't let his simple attire deceive you. He's an important liaison."

"I see. The government's thinking about painting the secret facility a different color?"

"Nikki suggested a rainbow."

"Nikki's sweet. Are you two..."

"Friends," Jake says. "She's the little sister I never had. She needs to get a life. I keep throwing guys in front of her but none stick. She needs to find a nice guy, get married, and get out of this business."

"The business of... working for you?"

"Hollywood," he says.

"She said the acting thing didn't work out."

"It hardly ever does. What exactly is it that you do?"

I almost trip again from the expert misdirect. I recover. "That depends on the client. Everyone's a little different."

"We'll discuss," he says. "Let's get you settled into your room."

I FOLLOW JAKE UP THREE FLIGHTS OF WOODEN STAIRS, THE laughter and noise fading in the background. We walk down a long carpeted hallway until we reach a room tucked away at the very end. "Welcome to your slice of sanity." He inserts an old-fashioned key in the lock, opens the door, and gestures for me to enter first.

I walk in. The suite is bigger than my living room. There are whitewashed plank floors, white walls, and a white wrought iron bed sits in a far corner. Large, overstuffed furniture – a sofa, a loveseat, a few chairs casually rest here inviting occupants to sit back and take in the view over a canyon.

Jake walks to the window and pushes the paned glass open a few inches. "Come here," he says.

I stand next to him. A breeze wafts in carrying hints of sage, eucalyptus, and citrus.

"What do you see?"

"A gorgeous, spread out city with pockets of country. Bright lights, broken up with slices of canyon darkness. A ginormous, glorious mish-mash."

"Yup," he says. "L.A.'s funny. When I first got here I thought I'd never call this place home. Home would always be New Mexico."

"Do you still feel that way?"

"I don't know. It's been fourteen years. Sometimes L.A. feels like home. Sometimes it doesn't. I'm not quite sure if I belong here or not."

A look comes over him. Something haunted.

Traces of something stir in me. My heart beats faster. Not from excitement. Not from anticipation. From fear. Unease twists in my gut. I'm finally picking up on Jake. I'm just not exactly sure what I'm picking up on. "Hey," I say and touch his shoulder.

He blinks, looks down at my hand, and I can practically see his subconscious retreating. "I'm waxing all nostalgic and you probably think, 'Jeez this guy's an entitled douche. Can't he just give me a little privacy and some downtime?'"

"I was *not* thinking that."

"Maybe you should be." He grabs my suitcases. "Where do you want your bags?"

"I'll do that."

"It's part of your Welcome to L.A. night," he says. "Take me up on it. I'll probably never be this nice again."

"I doubt that. Closet?"

"Closet it is."

I stare out at the lights below. I've only been in L.A. a few hours and I already know the problem isn't going to be that Jake Keller's thoughtless or an asshole. The problem is he's good-hearted, laid back, and kind. He went from warm to nostalgic to guarded in ten seconds flat. Not enough to give me emotional whiplash but fast enough for me to take notice.

Jake Keller fits the profile of the perfect victim. The guy people take advantage of. Someone with crazy talent who in spite of his being a smart-ass is generally trustworthy. The kind of person a predator, narcissistic asshole takes advantage of.

I can almost see the writing on the wall. Someone screwed this guy over and he's shutting down because that is the only way he knows how to survive. My determination to help him, heal him, is renewed. Now it's just a matter of getting comfortable in his life, making him comfortable with me, cracking him open, finding the wound, dissecting it out like the alien he joked about.

This would be three years worth of work for your average shrink. I wish I boasted a doctorate in psychology but I don't. I'm just a 21st Century Courtesan and I need to crack this man open in a few weeks to a month. It doesn't matter that I'm tired. I need to shower, change clothes, and get to work. Healing waits for no one.

He reappears. "Want anything? Food, clothes, help making the bed? Although the maid shows up a few times a day. You have a private bathroom. Everything's in there should you have forgotten anything in your travels. And," he fumbles in his pocket and hands me a keyring. "Here's your key."

"Thank you."

"See you downstairs?"

"Absolutely. I'll freshen up and be right down."

"Things are going to get busy around here. Got a new movie coming out. In case I forget to tell you." He looks at me. His eyes sweet. His lips full. Something about the way the smell of citrus mixing with lavender as it sifts through my room smells like hope mixed with dreams mixed with heartache.

"What?" Somewhere in the mish-mash of Jake's emotions, somewhere in this juxtaposition of city and country, lying deep within the slashes that separate bright and dark is a real man, a real hero, not just an image projected onto a screen. A chill of determination spreads down my arms because I know this isn't going to be an easy ride. I know shit has happened to him. But I also know I am determined to find him.

"Thanks for coming to L.A. to help me," he says. "I appreciate it." He turns and leaves the room, the door clicking shut behind him.

———

THE MEGA-SHOWER IN MY BATHROOM HAS SIX HEADS WITH rotating jets. It pulses hot, throbbing water on my too tight shoulders and I lean into their beat. The jets pummel the sore area between my shoulder blades that seized up last night after I found the box of hair on my bed. After I discovered some asshole had violated me.

In my rush to get here I had placed being violated on the sidelines. But here they are demanding attention, their jagged edges begging to be butterflied back together. The problem is when you're a caregiver, too frequently you put your own needs on the back burner.

'Bad news. The violation's not going to go away overnight,' Queasy says.

'Good news. Jake Keller's a decent guy. You'll figure out what broke him. Relax,' Hope says.

I stretch my shoulders, my ribs, and my back. I lean against the pretty sea-colored mosaic tiles. I dial up the jets to strong, the water pummeling me as I shake off the jet lag and wake the hell up. I'm still on central time, but two hours isn't that huge of a difference.

When it dawns on me my weariness might be more from the violation and less from the time change. The water pulses on the small of my back and the tight muscles finally relent. If Dylan never gets around to asking me to marry him, I swear I'm going to propose to this shower and slip a ring on it.

I turn off the faucet and reluctantly step out. I grab a bath sheet, dry off, and wrap it around me. I sample from the variety of body moisturizers on a shelf built into the wall. The first smells of vanilla. The next lemon. The third something herbal, more intriguing. I pick number three, pour the concoction in my palm. I drop the bath sheet, and smooth the lotion over my warm skin. Grabbing the towel from the floor I dry off my hair and walk back to my bedroom.

A man is standing there.

"Nice to finally meet the girl with the magic touch," he says.

❧ 5 ❧

PRETTY DOLL

PRETTY DOLL

ADAM, THE METRO GUY FROM THE PARTY SITS ON THE BED in front of me. I'm naked and his gaze roams over me. He creeps me out.

"Have we been introduced?" I ask, wrapping the towel tightly around me. "Or is this the part where I call security?"

"No need to call security, darling. This is the part where you thank me for getting you this job. I'm Adam Bachman. Jake's producing partner."

"Call me Evelyn." I walk cautiously into the bedroom instructing the goose bumps on my body to calm the hell down. I can handle loose boundaries guy. I've handled his type before. Besides, if he puts a hand on me he'll get two fingers in his eye so fast he'll be lucky if he sees again. "Awesome meeting you," I say. "I thought Ray Stark hired me."

"I was the one who talked him into it." He pats the bed

next to him. Upon closer reflection he's patting clothes laid out on the bed.

My clothes. Jeans. A cute top, and a nude bra.

'Crap,' Queasy says.

After what happened yesterday maybe I should make a run for it. But adrenaline, the bitch queen of fight and flight, smacks a 12-gauge needle into my heart. It's all I can do not to punch this guy. "You're making me uncomfortable, Adam." I lift my chin and pick up the clothes.

"Sorry."

But he's not sorry. He watches me too intently. He's looking for a reaction. He's sizing me up, waiting to see how I'll handle his indiscretion. My heart's pounding like the drums in a symphony's big finale. My cheeks warm with blood flooding into them but he could mistake that for me just stepping out of the shower. "I'm going to bet, Adam, you're not sorry because you let yourself into this room uninvited."

"Good call," he says.

There's no sexual vibe between us. He regards me like I'm a pretty doll stuffed onto a shelf that suddenly decided to speak.

"How did you get in here?"

"Jake gave me a key to this suite a few years back when I crashed here after a bad breakup."

I head to the walk-in closet where Jake left my suitcase. The lid is open, the contents neat, but re-arranged: the tops mixed in with the skirts and pants. I drop the towel and shrug on the clothes he picked out.

"Whatever you think you know about me rethink that," I say. "I'm here on business. No time for games."

'For fuck's sakes,' Queasy says executing flip-flops in my stomach. *'Cop an attitude or he'll continue dicking you around.'*

"Is this how you normally treat Jake's business associates?"

I ask. "You're a liability, dude. Jake will dump your trespassing ass."

"He'll never do that. Besides, we've been best friends since we were kids."

"He has handlers."

I walk through the suite to the bathroom without meeting his eyes. "Handlers realize when best friends who are producing partners have worn out their welcome. And then they handle it."

'*Snaps,*' Queasy says.

I open my makeup bag, squeeze foundation onto my fingers, blending it on my face and wonder how long it will take Mr. No Boundaries to join me in the bathroom. *Three, two, one...*

He hoists himself up on the blue and yellow patterned Spanish pavers that comprise the countertop. "I'm doing you a favor, Cookie. Melody and her posse were laying bets you'd come downstairs wearing something tragically inappropriate."

"The thirsty brunette with the too short skirt?" I dab on blush because I could use some color and I need to keep my hands moving cause they're still a little shaky. I also need to get downstairs and go to work. I'm not getting paid a fortune to relax in a swanky suite with sweeping views of L.A. I didn't travel 2000 miles to play petty power politics with Adam No Boundaries Bachman.

"The same," he says. "They'd snap pictures of you wearing what they thought was basic, or last year. They'd post that shit everywhere, try and shame you before you even hit the ground running."

"Good to know the welcome wagon's up and running." I swipe on eyeshadow, then liner, the shake in my hands evening out because I'm starting to feel like Adam's not going to hurt me. He's just going to irritate me to death one detail at a time.

"Letting myself in was an intervention, really," he says. "An act of kindness. I checked in on you in the shower. You seemed to be enjoying yourself, so I took the liberty of picking out your clothes for tonight's party. FYI, I might be an ass, but I'd never do anything to hurt Jake."

'Admirable,' Queasy says. *'Ditch this loser.'*

'Learn something,' Hope says. *'Then release him to his higher good.'*

I reach for my mascara but Adam beats me to the punch, handing me the tube. "Thank you," I say.

"Welcome."

I brush it on. "Besides the wardrobe advice, why are you here?"

"I wanted to talk with you alone. Explain Jake's situation. Obviously, I heard about you through people that travel in big money circles."

"Yes?" I drag styling crème through my hair.

"You help powerful men figure out the thing that screwed them up. You spend time with them, get to know them. Eventually you fuck them and they have a mysterious, magical breakthrough. Get their mojo back. And I thought if it works for those other guys, why not Jake?"

"But it *doesn't* work like that." I sigh. "There is no magic bullet. Besides, I'm not required to have sex with my clients. It's not a given."

"Get out. Sex isn't a given?"

"No. I'm not a prostitute." I walk out of the bathroom and pluck sexy slingbacks from my open suitcase. I sit on the bed and put on the shoes. "I decide who I do what with. And honestly? I'm damn picky."

He plunks down next to me. "How do you justify being picky considering the money you're paid?"

"How do you justify trespassing into my room? How do you justify talking Ray Stark into hiring me?"

"Do you know how many people Ray's hired to help Jake Keller?"

"No."

"Me neither. I've lost count. There was the yoga guru – Baba What's His Name. He downward dogged Jake, opened his chakras, taught him how to chant Sanskrit."

"Yoga can be healing," I say. My phone pings wildly.

"Healing. Ha. Right," He rakes a hand through his cropped auburn hair.

Mr. No Boundaries' bravado is melting like a sno cone dropped on a sidewalk on a hot summer day.

"Jake nailed his audition for the guy who traveled to India, lived in the slums for two years, and was enlightened. Then he started a tech company, became a zillionaire, and opened free health clinic for the poor."

"Good for him," I say, staring at my phone. My sister has texted. Oh, man, I hope everything's fine with Mom.

"Jake turned the part down," Adam said. "He turned down a ten million dollar acting fee because he didn't 'feel like it.' It wasn't 'in him.'"

Ruby: *Luke went back to his wife.*

"Oh," I say. "I take it this is an ongoing problem?"

"Yes. It's one of the reasons why you're here," Adam says.

"Got it," I say scrolling on my phone.

Evie: *I'm sorry. There will be more guys. I promise.*

Ruby: *Luke told me they were definitely divorcing.*

"I was shocked when Jake took the priest role in The Messenger movie," Adam says. "Considering everything that went down when we were kids."

"Right," I say.

Ruby: He told me that a hundred times.

Evie: It's not easy.

This flurry of texts is all about Ruby's love life. No reference to Mom which means she's okay, thank God. I know she's not thrilled I delayed our vacation. Change can set her off.

Ruby: He even met with an attorney.

Evie: I'm sorry, honey. I'm working. Can we talk about this IRT on the phone soon?

Ruby: Yes. Whatever.

"The nutritionist to the stars thought Jake's indecision was due to chemical imbalances in his diet," Adam says. "He taught Jake how to make kale smoothies."

"Kale's awesome." I check my next message.

Amelia: How's it going in L.A.?

Amelia: Is Movie Star as hot as we think?

Evie: Going OK.

Evie: Yeah, GF - super hot!

Evie: Especially his ass.

"Apparently kale's good for everything except fixing Jake,"

he says. "The nutritionist to the stars tried but failed."

There's something wistful in Adam's tone. He's looking more and more like a lost puppy and I'm starting to not hate him.

Evie: *In the middle of work. Talk later?*

Amelia*: 'K. Have a great time.*

Amelia: *Don't forget your roots.*

Evie*: Had my hair done before I left.*

Amelia: *Not those roots, weirdo.*

Amelia: *You know -- where you're from.*

Evie: *If I forget where I'm from I'm sure you'll tell me how to get back there.*

Amelia: *Ha.*

Evie: *Chat tomorrow?*

Amelia: *Can't wait to hear all!*

I shove the phone in my jeans back pocket. "I need to work," I say, snagging the key from the bureau. I stop at the door and look back at Adam who now looks like a puppy that's been abandoned in the rain. Sad eyes, droopy shoulders.

"Come on," I say. "Let's go. There's beer and pizza downstairs."

"Hear me out." He stands. "You're another consultant.

Another hired hand to help Jake. Whatever it is that you do, please be the one that fixes him."

"I'll do my best."

"I hate seeing him like this. I haven't seen him like this in a long time. Whatever this thing is, it's ripping him up."

"I'll try, Adam." I hold the door open and he follows me into the hallway. I shut the door behind us and check the lock. "I want my key back," I say, holding out my hand.

He pulls it from his pocket and places it in my palm. "I'm sorry."

I could hold onto my anger longer. After all, he trespassed. He crossed boundaries. He was an asshole. But I called his bluff, he took a few steps back, and this is a step toward détente. "Apology accepted. But you're buying the beer."

❧ 6 ❧

SHARK EYES

SHARK EYES

DOWNSTAIRS THE PARTY'S STILL POPPING. ADAM PLUCKS A cold brew from the refrigerator, cracks it open, and hands it to me.

"Adam!" A dark-haired, nerdy, cute guy wearing trendy glasses waves from the hallway.

Adam waves back then says to me, "I need to talk to him."

"Go," I say. "Do you know where I can find Jake?"

"He's either in the family room or in his office."

"And they are located where?"

"Family room's down the hall. Office is in a bungalow behind the pool. He hides out there a lot lately."

"Thanks."

"Catch you later, Cookie. If you need anything mention my name."

I WANDER INTO THE FAMILY ROOM. MELODY, THE JEALOUS brunette with the too short skirt is with her posse standing next to an old-fashioned juke box. They talk behind raised hands, barely covering checking me out. No doubt they're judging my outfit. No doubt they're finding something wrong with it. Slender pins of jealousy prick my skin and I imagine slipping on a Teflon coat. Undoubtedly, they'd judge that 'last year' as well.

Nikki's playing pool with a few guys at the far end of the room. They're all laughing. Her hair's down, she's unbuttoned the top buttons on her crisp white shirt and has ditched her shoes. She's leaning over the pool table aiming at the eight ball, killing it with the guys who look like they're in love with her.

I get a feeling Nikki doesn't allow herself a lot of down time. I don't want to interrupt her happiness. Don't want to make her think she's got to take care of any more business tonight. I keep edging through the crowd. Floor to ceiling French doors open to a wide backyard. I stare out at the twinkling Italian lights strung at intervals high above the lawn.

A nine-foot wrought iron fence surrounds the property, which abruptly drops off into a dark canyon. Tucked in a far corner is a pristine, rectangular cobalt blue pool with tea lights resting on saucers floating on the surface. The glow is magical against the blue of the pool and the black of the canyon. A bungalow sits at the edge of the property. Through the drawn shades there's a soft glow from a lamp.

Stepping outside, the music's softer, the night air carries a cool breeze scented with cedar logs and pine. Flames flicker in a fire pit to my left. A silver-haired man and a curvy woman sit close to it, nursing drinks and carrying on an animated discussion. I recognize the woman. She's Jake's publicist, Pinkie Stein. Streaks of her signature fuchsia and silver strands woven through her Champagne-colored, shoulder-length hair.

"You need to stop crowding him, Ray," Pinkie says. "Stop hiring experts. Stop pushing people at him. He'll figure it out."

"This is the last one. Promise," Ray says. "I let Adam talk me into it in a moment of weakness. 'Everyone who's anyone's talking about this girl,' he said. I researched and he was right."

"Like who?" Pinkie asks.

"Dominic Butler from VMI Music was bleeding money. Busted his ass left, right, and center, and still couldn't score a hit for two years. He didn't know if he was picking the wrong songs, or over-producing or under-producing the tunes. He second guessed himself so much he started calling his fiancée by his girlfriend's name and vice versa."

"Yikes," Pinky says. "Messy."

"Yeah, that didn't go over all that well. They both dumped him and kept the jewelry as well as the cars."

"I remember when TMZ broke that one. Tell me more."

"Dominic hired this girl, the one who's coming here to help Jake. She moved in with him for a few weeks. Figured out his problem had nothing to do with music. That Dominic had lost his mojo back in high school when his parents split up. For some reason he felt responsible that he couldn't make their marriage work. He sucked up all that energy and internalized it. He was doing the same thing in his business twenty-five years later. Repeating the pattern. Not realizing his past was running him."

"This girl," Pinkie says. "She broke him open, helped him have an epiphany?"

"Yes," Ray says. "Once Dominic realized where it was coming from he moved on that knowledge. He stopped taking responsibility for what wasn't his. Got his shit together, figured out his brand. He produced the right artists with the right songs. Did what he knew in his gut would work. Bam – it did. Bam – he won a handful of Grammys last year. Bam – he's back on track and his bank account proves it."

"What do we know about this woman you hired?"

"Astronomically priced call girl," Ray says. "An operation out of Chicago. For all I know it's mob related. Wouldn't that make for great fucking tabloid headlines. 'JAKE KELLER CONSORTING WITH MOB PROSTITUTE!'"

My heart twists in my chest at the same time my stomach nosedives and my self-respect splatters in bloody bits across the pavement.

"Ma Maison?" Pinkie asks.

"How did you know?"

"I'm in PR. Ma Maison has a few girls who specialize in tough cases. These women are rumored to be excellent at what they do. The rest are average. Did you get one of the good ones?"

"What do you mean?"

I'm not sure if I'm one of "the good ones," average ones, or bad ones because I'm feeling dirty. Shamed. I turn and head to the bungalow. The light shines through the thick fabric, glowing around the edges. I take a deep breath, take a moment to center, ground, and pray.

Dear God.

I made it here safe and sound, thank You. Thought I'd get you up to speed. It seems that Jake has a fair number of people around him with their own agendas. Help me to remember that I've only got one: Crack Jake Keller open. Track down what hurt him. Expose that lie. I'm here to help him heal. Get the poison out. I appreciate any help, God. Any guidance you can throw my way. And this I ask for in the name of the Father and the Son and the Holy Spirit. Amen.

I cross myself then spot a glimpse of Jake through a gap

between the blind and the window frame. He shuts down his computer and grabs keys from the desktop. Do I knock? Do I not knock? Do I just hover here indecisively like some creepy stalker?

Wait. Hold up. What am I doing? I am totally spying on this guy. I'm invading his personal space. Sure, I didn't stride in unannounced and rifle through his underwear drawer, but I'm still being an asshole. Ugh, this is not who I am.

I step away from the bungalow, and make my way back toward the pool. I wasn't hired to be a peeping Tom. I certainly don't like it when folks invade my privacy.

Jake strides out of the bungalow. and makes his way toward the house. He doesn't see me.

"Jake!" I call.

He doesn't turn. I don't think he heard me over the noise of the party. I start to follow him when someone squeezes my arm. I know before I even turn around that the person who has me in his firm grasp has a smooth, large, cool palm and a steel grip. He means business. "Evelyn?"

I swivel and look up into cold eyes. The eyes of a shark. Eyes that only want one thing.

"Yes?"

"Ray Stark."

"I know."

"Is peeking into windows going to help you peer inside Jake Keller's soul?"

"I don't know... No... Let go of me." I shake free from his grasp, but probably only because he allows me to.

"Glad you're here. We need to discuss your strategy," he says, his breath growing rapid, his nostrils flaring. "There's a lot riding on this."

"Right. I hear you. But now's not the time for strategizing."

I hustle away from him because Jake's already disappearing from my sight, stepping back inside the house.

"Evelyn!" Ray calls after me but I don't even break stride.

By the time I set foot in the kitchen a sweat's broken out on my forehead. Adam's still schmoozing with the guy with glasses. "Where's Jake?" I ask.

He points to the laundry room. I edge as fast as I can through the crowd that's thinning out. I trip over one of the baskets filled with clothes, and catch myself on the washing machine. An engine revs. I throw open the garage door. Jake, on his motorcycle, is rumbling out onto the street. I call after him again, but he's already peeling off. He disappears around a curve in the road.

So much for strategy.

So much for healing.

I turn and head back to my room.

I TURN ON THE TV, CHECK MESSAGES, AND AN HOUR LATER I'm so tired my eyes are swimming. I scrub off my makeup, pull on my jammies, and open the window.

A soft breeze wafts in, carrying hints of lavender and rose petals. It's nothing like the muggy summer Chicago air around my condo that smells like garbage spiked with urine. Outside a vine of white roses trails up to my window. I collapse back onto the queen-sized feather top bed, and snuggle under the light down comforter.

A low but persistent *knock-knock-knock* on my door startles me awake. The clock on the side table reads a little after 2 a.m. It's probably Adam Mr. No Boundaries wanting to spend the night again. "Go away," I say. "We'll talk later."

"Okay," a guy says, but it's not Adam Bachman. It's Jake Keller and my heart practically leaps out of my chest. I vault out of the bed, open the door and peer out. Jake is stumbling down the hallway, his arms out-stretched, ping-ponging between opposite walls in an attempt to steady himself. He's treading that thin line between medium drunk and super drunk. "Hey," I say. "What's up?"

"Nothing. It's too late," he says and waves one hand dismissively. "Or maybe too early. Shouldn't have knocked. Sorry."

I glance down at my PJs. I didn't plan on sharing my "I love Queen's Falafels" T-shirt with short shorts in public. I hustle down the hallway, just in time to see Jake lean against a wall and slide down it. "It's not too late," I say. "What's going on?"

"Thought we could talk. Probably not the smartest, the best, I mean, not a good idea."

"We can talk," I say.

"Easy for you to say. In case you haven't noticed, I'm a little drunk."

"Get out," I say and grin.

He grins back. A sloppy smile but sweet nonetheless. "I knew from the second I saw you that nothing would get past you."

I hold out a hand to him. "Lots of things get past me."

He takes my hand. "I have a problem, Evie."

"What's the problem?" I hoist him up.

He sways and points in one direction, then the other. "Your room's that way. Mine's the other."

"Got it." I place a steadying hand on his arm. "So, what's the actual problem?"

"I'm lost." He looks up at me with those eyes. Those eyes that could talk a girl into doing just about anything.

"You want me to help you find your room? I don't know where it is but I bet I can figure that out."

"Not the room I'm worried about. Don't care 'bout the

damn room," he says. "It's everything else. Everything else is just too much and there's nothing I can do about it. I've tried."

He's melting down. But drunken meltdowns usually don't reveal all that much. They're just messy. "What have you tried?" I ask.

"Booze. Therapy. Working too hard. Sleeping pills. Fucking the wrong girls. Gardening. Exercise. Weed. Therapy. Oh, and potato chips."

"I see. Is there anything you haven't tried?"

"Yes," he says. "You. Can I sleep with you tonight?"

❧ 7 ❧

A THOUSAND TEARS

A THOUSAND TEARS

———

BACK IN MY ROOM I TRY NOT TO WATCH AS JAKE UNZIPS HIS jeans, yanks them off and tosses them. God help me I see that perfect ass up close and personal. As much as I try to avert my eyes, I'd lay money there's not a butt implant to be found in this room.

He collapses, half naked, on my bed with a thunk, and rips off his T-shirt, arms flailing. And now *all* the goods are on display. And yes, they are magnificent. His body is every bit as tight and taught and ripped as every girl, guy, and grand-mother might imagine.

"Evie," he says. "Don't take this the wrong way. I overdid it."

"Everyone's been there."

"I don't feel so good. I think I'm just going to hit the sack tonight."

"That works for me."

He reaches for the comforter but he's managed to tangle it around his ankles. "Help, please."

I wrangle the covers over him, trying not to stare at his sculpted chest that's distracted me in movies, TV, and on magazine stands. Trying not to stare at everything else male and magnificent on display.

'Focus, Evie,' Hope says.

'You try and focus, bitch,' Queasy snaps.

I try to find anything else in the room that looks interesting. Aha. The plump loveseat in the alcove next to the window looks super comfy. Now that Jake's in my bed I can sleep on that.

"Evie." Jake pats the bed. "Sit with me."

I do.

"I'm not really a drinker," he says. "Just had a bad night."

"I can tell." Dear God, this man is handsome.

"Nikki said you were really nice. Adam said you'll figure out what's wrong with me."

"I'll do my best."

"I'd be grateful. Have you ever felt lost? Turned around?"

"Yes." He has no idea how many times.

"Did you ever figure it out?" He looks at me with those eyes.

"I'm working on that." I soothe a wayward lock of hair off his forehead.

"Sleep with me, Evie." He pats the pillow next to him. "Only sleep. Nothing else. Promise."

I lie down facing him when I'm struck by how surreal this moment is. I'm a girl from Chicago with a crazy Mom and a sister with a bad boyfriend picker. I'm an escort —assumed to be a prostitute. Holy shit on a shingle, how many people would kill to be in my position?

"Evie." Jake traces a finger across my face, down my neck and out of nowhere my breath grows raspy, my throat thickens, and I can't breathe. The sadness of a thousand tears fills my throat, threatening to tear me to pieces.

"Ray said this is costing us a fortune. He says you'd better be worth it," Jake says. "But, you know, Ray can be a giant dick."

I am the casket at the bottom of a freshly dug grave suffocating in dirty truths that must be revealed or they will bury me. Panic, shock, anger and fear hijack my breath, smothering me with despair. Jake's despair. It blisters from my throat, oozing shame. Its roots twist through my chest, snake into my heart, and then disappear deep inside me. I know that this despair is an empathic reaction. And yet it breaks my heart that it belongs to Jake.

'Breathe, Evie,' Queasy says.

'Breathe,' Hope says.

If I can ride this out, if I can hold onto his pain, maybe I can figure out where it came from. Maybe I can figure out what or who hurt him. Determine the words that Jake needs to say. The words that will set him free.

He kisses me softly then presses a finger to my lower lip. "I'm sorry about tonight, Evie. Sorry for interrupting you so late. Sorry for... thanks for letting me stay." He closes his eyes and within seconds he's asleep.

I stare at the ceiling counting my inhales and exhales as the minutes tick by. My breath is raspy and desperate, like an old man on a ventilator clinging to the last bits of life. But I know now where the poison exists in Jake's body. It's in his throat. It's in his chest. And I know that I can find it again and figure out whatever it is that's shutting him down. And then I can help him heal.

Maybe I'm the girl who's wearing something basic.

Maybe I'm the girl who is shamed for being an escort.

And maybe I'll be the girl who saves the fucking day.

THE FOLLOWING MORNING THE SUN'S SHINING THROUGH the windows. I am alone in the bed. Jake is gone. Sleep has this way of re-setting the machine. Jake was drunk last night, drowning in booze and sadness. If he was dating Ruby I'd tell her to be careful. But he's not dating my sister, nor is he dating me. He's my client. I'm a professional, and this is a job, pure and simple.

I shower, get dressed, and grab my phone. Messages ping through, the last from Dylan McAlister. High stakes poker player. Former church baby. Along with his brother, one of the heirs to the throne of the Lighthouse Cathedral empire. My part-time boyfriend, the man I fell in love with almost two years ago, and the guy who keeps threatening to put a ring on my finger but doesn't, hasn't – whatever – because according to him the timing isn't right.

I had a gig in Mexico about six months ago and scheduled a long layover when I flew through Dallas so I could spend some time with Dylan's mom. I love Rosemary McAlister. She's a feisty, sixty-something, take-no-bullshit woman who's been battling breast cancer for a few years. She met me at a bar close to the airport where we sat next to each other in a little booth and talked for a couple of hours.

"Dylan's starting to piss me off," Rosemary said. "Maybe I shouldn't say anything, but I consider myself somewhat entitled. I'm the only mother he'll ever have."

"Truth," I said. "What's wrong?"

"It's been over a year since you two met. I was hoping he'd have slipped a sizable, pretty ring on your finger by now."

"Dylan does things his way," I said. "There's no forcing him to do anything he's not ready to do."

"He's taking his good, old sweet time," she said. "He always gives me a cashmere sweater for Christmas, a fruit basket, and gift certificates. Do you think I can exchange those for you as my new daughter-in-law?"

"Ha!"

"Are you going to put the fear of God into him or do you want me to?"

"You," I said, and tried to cover a smile. But Rosemary McAlister wasn't the kind of person you could easily hide smiles or anything else from, which is why it threw me when she grabbed my hand and squeezed it.

"Promise me one thing, Evie," she said.

"Anything."

"Don't wait for Dylan. If someone else comes along who loves you as fiercely but is willing to commit I want you to go for it."

"Oh, Rosemary," I said. "That's not going to happen."

"I have a feeling. Promise me. But only if you love him."

"Only if I love him," I said. "I promise."

And as much I do love Dylan McAlister, I refuse to wait for him. He knows it and he's not all that happy about it.

Dylan: *I'm calling you. Pick up.*

Evie: *No. I'm working.*

Dylan: *I miss you.*

Evie: *I miss you back.*

Dylan: *When are you done with this job?*

Evie: *Few weeks to a month.*

Dylan: *How about after you're done I visit you in Chicago?*

Evie: Yes, please.

Dylan: Wait... Mom says you should come here.

Dylan: Texas.

Dylan: Mom misses you.

My heart sinks. He's right. Rosemary's the mother I always wanted and she's going through another round of treatment.

Evie: I miss her back. Gotta go.

Dylan: Phone sex, baby?

Evie: Fuck you, baby. No.

Dylan: That's what I was asking about.

Evie: Keep dreaming, player...

Ping–ping–ping more texts come in.

Ruby: Where are you?

Evie: Working. What's up?

Ruby: Mom's been hiding her pills.

Evie: What?!! Why?

Ruby: Don't know.

Ruby: Her doctor called me. Wanted to know if I knew why she'd be acting out.

Aw crap.

Evie: I wonder if it's because I canceled our trip?

Ruby: Don't know.

Ruby: Don't worry about that.

Ruby: You can't control everything, right?

Evie: Right.

Ruby: I'm going up there in a week. You might want to do that too.

Evie: As soon as I'm done with this job.

Ruby: Where are you this time?

Evie: You know the drill— not supposed to disclose.

Ruby: Right. Okay, Batgirl.

Evie: Not Batgirl. I wish. Talk soon.

I HEAD TO THE KITCHEN AND POUR MYSELF A CUP OF coffee. Nikki wanders in wearing a rumpled T-shirt and sweats, looking like she just rolled out of bed.

"Jake around?" I ask.

"As far as I know he's up and out," she says pouring herself a bowl of cereal.

"He rolled in last night around 2 a.m." I say.

"He does that a lot lately," she says, spooning down break‑ fast. "Ever since he shut down. Do you want some cereal? Sorry. That was rude of me not to ask."

I point to my bowl of berries and yogurt. "I'm good, thanks. Do you know where he goes?"

She shakes her head. "I asked him a month or so ago. He wouldn't tell me. I assume typical guy stuff."

"I Googled the hell out of him before I flew out here, and to be honest, I couldn't find all that much credible information."

"Did you see the thing in the *Inquirer* about him fathering the alien baby?" She makes a face.

"Truth! Baby looked just like him. Jake's mom died a few years back. She wasn't that old. Is that part of the problem?"

"Nancy was a piece of work," Nikki says. "They adored each other. She was a smoker. He tried to get her to quit for years but she wouldn't. Sudden heart attack."

"Is he still grieving?"

"He'll grieve forever," she says. "But no, I don't think that's it."

"His girlfriend of two years ran off with a director."

"The lovely Jacqueline. She met the guy on an indie movie a few years back. He was ten years younger than her and smoking hot. I would have fucked him three ways to Thursday."

I blink. "Hotter than Jake?"

She laughs. "Hot in a different way. They're living in Provence, now. It threw Jake for about a month. He worked out a lot and banged about a hundred girls. I used to tease him that his dick was going to break."

I cover a smile. "Did it?"

"I haven't seen it, so I don't know."

I saw it last night in passing and it looked just fine, if a bit on the substantial size.

Adam walks into the kitchen, throws his keys on the counter, and heads for the coffee pot.

"Morning sunshine," Nikki says.

"Talk to me after caffeine," he says. "Jake here?"

"Nope. Maybe he's working out."

"We've got that meeting with Howard from Tru Blue..."

"Jake mentioned something last night about postponing the Tru Blue meeting," Nikki says.

"I've postponed it twice," Adam says downing his coffee. "Howard's going to think we're dicking him around."

"Not my call," Nikki says.

"Right." He plucks his phone from his back pocket and begins typing.

"Business as usual?" Nikki asks.

"More like business that never gets done now that Jake keeps changing plans," Adam says.

I raise my hand. "Is there anything I can..."

"Yes," Adam says and scowls at me. "Do your job. Spend some time with Jake. figure out what's wrong. Fix him."

"Um..."

"Douche nozzle." Nikki throws a berry at his head. "Evie's been here under 24 hours. You know how Jake is. He's here, he's there. He's oh so sweet."

"Super sweet," I say.

"Then he does his imitation of 'The Shadow' and splits," she says. "It's not like Evie can rendition him and get the job done. Hey... Not a bad idea?"

I shake my head. "I suck at rendition-ing."

"We'll do that another day," Nikki says. "I'm supposed to entertain you for a few hours. Jake's joining us after."

"He's goofing off instead of taking the meeting with Tru Blue?" Adam asks.

"You can't have it both ways," Nikki says. "Unless Evie's clairvoyant, she's going to have to spend time with him."

"Fine," He grumbles.

"Sounds good," I say. "What are we doing?"

"It's L.A. We've got the beach. Beverly Hills. History. Studio Tour. Theme parks. Boats. Surfing. Shopping. Farmer's market. Whatever you want. Pick your poison. We've got a lot here."

"I want it all," I say, nearly spilling my coffee.

"Yay! The All Access Pass tour," Nikki says. "My favorite."

"I'm coming with," Adam says.

8

NOT A REGULAR GIRL

NOT A REGULAR GIRL

OVER THE NEXT FIVE DAYS I LEARNED HOW TO SURF AT Topanga Beach.

Jake showed up in time to watch me stand up on the board for the first time and ride a wave to shore. Nikki and one of the guys crushing on her took me to a theme park. Jake showed up wearing a ball cap and shades. Later that night we hit a Dodgers game.

Five days later he leaves work early and we go to the Grand Central market, a cornucopia of food booths, housed in the hustle and bustle of downtown L.A. We sit at a little counter in front of two guys in chef uniforms cooking Vietnamese seafood and noodle dishes on a range.

"I'm not in the mood to gear up for a movie launch," Jake says. "But you know what is refreshing?"

"No. What?"

He takes my hand and strokes the back of it. "Except for

a handful of people no one knows about us. You and I have this thing, this friendship. I mean, technically you work for me. I know that."

"I know," I say, uninvited butterflies fluttering in my stomach.

"Do you ever wonder if it's more than work?"

He kisses my hand and I smile at him. "I'm not supposed to wonder about that."

"I'm wondering," he says. He leans in and kisses me, his full lips on mine, his hand on the back of my neck.

My heart bumps in my chest, and for a second I forget about healing him. I forget about his pain. I just kiss him back, just like that girl in the movie in the drowning rain.

WE PARK THE MOTORCYCLE IN THE GARAGE OF HIS SPANISH style house high above Sunset Boulevard.

"Hey," he says. "About that kiss."

"What about it?"

"First time we kissed in public. You okay with that?"

"Yes. You?"

"Yup." He holds open the door from the garage to the laundry room for me. "I'm pretty sure the crew here thinks more is going on than just kissing."

"I'd bet on that."

"Still, it's not like I want to open this up for discussion right now. Everyone dissects everything I do."

"No worries," I say.

I'm not delusional. I know we're not a couple, not in love. But we definitely like each other. There's a spark. If Jake was a regular guy and I was a regular girl we'd be dating. If we were in Chicago, we'd go to my favorite burger joints under the el. We'd take in more baseball games, cheer on the

Cubbies or the Sox, hit the bike path that winds along Lake Michigan, and race each other around all those pretty sailboats.

But he's not a regular guy and I'm not a regular girl. Which is why it's a little off-putting when Nikki screeches as we walk into the kitchen.

"OMG there are pictures of you two posted on HotCelebs' Instagram page," she says. "They're being shared everywhere."

"They're hashtagging the new movie, Jake," Adam says. "Wondering who Evie is and if you met her on set. Hiring Evie is brill, man."

Jake's shoulders sag. "I had a great time," he whispers to me. "For what it's worth, today wasn't PR." He squeezes my hand, then heads to the backyard.

"Jake!" I call after him but he doesn't even break stride.

"Sorry," Nikki mouths.

I walk into the backyard. The soft light flicks on in the bungalow. I make my way around the pool. Jake shuts down his laptop, drops his head in his hands then grabs his keys. He's leaving again. I can feel it. He's retreating into the field of hurt and I can't reach him right now because if I push too hard I'll just push him away.

I ball up my feelings and march back inside the house. I know more about him than I did a week ago. I like him more than I did a week ago. I hear his bike rev and peel out of the garage. It tears me up a little more than it did when I first got here.

"You hungry?" Nikki asks.

"Nope. I'm going to call it an early night."

"I'm sorry," she says.

"Me too."

THERE'S A *KNOCK-KNOCK-KNOCK* ON MY DOOR AND I STARTLE awake. I look at the clock on the side table. It's 2 a.m.

"It's me," Jake says from the hallway.

I get up and open the door. He smells of incense, frankincense, and sage. His eyes are clear. "Are you okay?"

"No," he says. "I wanted to say I'm sorry for leaving like that. I wanted you to know I'm not drunk. That's all." He turns and walks away.

"Stay," I call after him. "I'd like it if you stayed."

❧ 9 ❧

LUCKY ME

LUCKY ME

———

JAKE ENTERS MY ROOM, AND SHUTS THE DOOR QUIETLY behind him. He pulls me toward him, wraps his arms around me, and kisses me.

He starts with my lips, brushing his against mine. He takes his time. Tasting, exploring, as our bodies get to know each other. He grows bolder, his tongue slipping inside my mouth. Goosebumps erupt on the backs of my arms. He pulls back, and glances into my eyes. Then he kisses my forehead, before moving his lips to my cheek. He runs his fingers through my hair, scraping his nails against my scalp and I arch under his touch. Shivers zip up my spine. My nipples pebble.

He reaches one firm hand behind my waist, and pulls me flush against him. I place my hand on his muscular chest, and caress it through his thin T-shirt. I move my hand to his shoulder, enjoying the definition in his muscles, then draw my hand up and down his arm. I practically will him to take off his shirt.

Lucky me.

I get my wish.

He tears off his T-shirt and drops it to the floor. His mouth is back on mine. I feel his arousal through his jeans. He's big, already hard, and he's growing even harder by the second. The V between my legs throbs and I grow wet.

"Evie," he says, exhaling, and walks me back toward the bed.

I breathe him in, practically melting under his touch.

He grazes his lips against the soft skin of my neck, and slips my nightshirt over my head before tossing it aside. The night air is cool, and goosebumps prickle on the backs of my arms. I am bare from the waist up, wearing only my cropped cotton pj bottoms that skim the tops of my thighs.

"Let me look at you." He leans back, his gaze traveling from my head to my toes. "Gorgeous," he says, palming my breast, before rolling the nipple between his thumb and forefinger.

Excitement courses through me like I've had a glass of Champagne. He moves his hand to my other breast, caresses it, then bends his head, and takes my nipple in his mouth and suckles it.

I groan. This man is sexy as sin.

When I have sex with a client, the first time is all about getting to know each other. I don't need to heal him in our first session. It's about trust and play, comfort and endorphins. It's about getting used to each other, seeing what he likes, him learning how to pleasure me.

But right now I cop to being oh so lustful for Jake Keller. I want more. I want to feel his hardness inside me. I want him to rock my world. I want to rock his. I place my hand on his waistband and look into his eyes for assurance.

"Yes," he says.

I run my hand over the bulge in his pants. He is throbbing with need. I unhook the metal button, pull the zipper slowly over his cock and take it in my hand. He's big and full and hard. I circle his dick with my hand mid-shaft. I slide my closed fist over the head and then back down, and repeat, stroking him faster.

He groans. "Hang on," he says and strips off his jeans.

Photos do not do this man justice. Jake Keller is beautiful naked. Six pack abs. Hard hips. Wide shoulders. A brush of hair on his arms and legs.

I kiss his mouth and he kisses me back slowly. He draws a hand down my body, skimming my breasts. My nipples harden.

"Your turn," he says, snagging the side of my PJ bottoms. He drags them down my leg.

I hold his shoulder and step out of them.

He looks at me appreciatively, a slight glaze to his eyes. His thick erection juts out from his pelvis. "You're so pretty, Evie." He grabs his jeans from the floor, and pulls a condom from his wallet. Ripping it open with his teeth, he rolls it on.

I wrap my arms around his neck. He walks me backward, his cock bumping against my pelvis. Butterflies flutter in my abdomen. My legs hit against the edge of the bed and we topple onto the cushy mattress.

He climbs on top of me, and edges himself between my legs. He runs his fingers over my sex, my folds, then back over my clit, and I squirm.

"So wet, Evie. So delicious." He slips a finger inside me and I arch under his touch. He slips in two fingers, then draws them out and pushes them back in.

I sigh. He is the fantasy. "I think you should be inside me for real."

"Not yet," he says. "We're still just getting to know each

other." He fucks me with two fingers, stroking the hard nub of my sex with his thumb as I rise under him, my back arching.

"Oh, Jake."

He places one hand on my pubic bone, pressing my pelvis into his other hand and I am under his control, under his fingers that I am learning are so talented. I buck against him, groaning. Thirty seconds later I have my first orgasm with him. Time flies away, tingles erupt over my body.

Moments later when I open my eyes he's grinning. "Good?"

"Good," I say and smile.

He kisses me, lines up the head of his cock against my sex, rubbing it back and forth against my wetness until he eases inside and I take him in.

I feel him deep in my core. He is warmth, and lust, and friendship, and kindness. I wrap my legs around his waist as he rocks into me. We find a rhythm. We find our way. Minutes later it's his turn to come, one hand on my breast, the other bracing himself against the mattress. "Evie! I'm coming." He shudders, his face contorting in pleasure.

He collapses against me, slick with sweat. I run my fingers through his hair and kiss his face. Eventually he falls asleep.

We've got a ways to go with healing — but I guarantee this is good start.

MESSY

MESSY

IT'S NON-STOP SEX FOR THREE DAYS.

Sex in the mornings. Sex in the shower. Sex in the afternoons. It's sex before, after, and sometimes during dinner. On the fourth morning, Jake leaves at dawn for an early morning magazine photo shoot. His movie's launching soon, there's a screening of it tomorrow night, and the PR machine is gearing up.

My phone pings.

Amelia: *How's it going?*

Evie: *Good.*

Amelia*: Excellent 'cause we're coming in town tomorrow.*

Evie*: Really?*

Evie: For what?

Amelia: Victoria has a gig. Some tech guy in town from China.

Evie: You?

Amelia: Tagging along for the bright lights and the shopping.

Amelia: Meet us for a coffee?

Evie: I think that works.

Evie: Hey – do you have time to pick up my mail?

Amelia: Yes, but I don't have a key.

Evie: My neighbor does –Hazel O'Rourke. I'll message you her contact info.

Evie: She's home all the time.

Amelia: Sounds good. I'll text you when we land.

———

SOMEONE WITH BIG MONEY IS PAYING THE TAB FOR Victoria because she's in a junior suite at the Ritz in Beverly Hills. An hour and a half later we're shopping on Melrose Avenue, poking our heads into little boutiques, and picking up trendy clothes and trinkets. Victoria charges them to her client's credit card. We stop at a French café and sit outside people watching, and eating an assortment of gluten free cakes.

"I wonder if I can learn how to do this empathy thing," Victoria muses.

"Probably," I say. "Sensitive people do it all the time without even knowing it."

"How does it work again?" Amelia asks.

"If I connect with a client, I feel in my body what he's feeling in his. I tune into his deepest, oldest fears."

"Messy," Victoria says. "Kink is cleaner."

"It is," I say. "And the knots are neater."

"After care's a bitch," Amelia says.

Victoria looks at her phone and stands up. "I've got to get ready for this date."

"Me too," Amelia says.

"I thought you were here for the shopping?" I say and order a ride.

"I am but I got a last minute gig," Amelia says. "Some movie producer. That's random in Hollywood – right? Hey, almost forgot." She pulls a letter out of her purse and hands it to me. "The only thing that wasn't junk mail. Let's talk tomorrow."

Tucked into the back seat of my ride, I open the letter.

Dear Evelyn:

I saw those pictures of you in *US Magazine* and shook my head. There you were with Jake Keller. The movie star, Jake Keller. Wow! Amazing!

First off, congratulations on scoring that opportunity. I have no idea how it landed in your lap but I guarantee you deserve it. Don't be humble shy about this. It's an accomplishment.

You are checking the boxes on your climb up the ladder by associating with famous people. Eventually people will be checking their own box by hanging out with you. That's a conversation we can have in the future should we ever meet up.

I suspect I freaked you out with my last gesture. My small present. The jewelry box. I didn't mean to alarm you, but I have to call it how I see it. You're a successful consultant but I knew you before that. I followed you in simpler times.

I'm still writing you via post. So old-fashioned of me, I know. Some things will never change. I miss the old days.

I only want your best, Evelyn.

I am, as always,

Your Devoted Fan

I SHIVER, SLIP IT BACK INSIDE THE ENVELOPE, AND TUCK IT into my purse.

JAKE'S MOVIE IS SCREENING IN A SMALL THEATRE ON THE studio lot. I sit in the middle of the center row. Jake's in the back talking to a few suits.

I text Victoria.

Evie: *I got another letter from the Fan.*

Evie: *He mentioned the jewelry box.*

Evie: *Should I report it to the cops?*

Victoria: *Yes. Talk later.*

The lights dim and Jake takes a seat next to me. He's biting his lip, trying not to glance around at the folks watching the screen. Ninety minutes later their verdict is in. The lights come up. People are clapping. He looks at me and smiles. "People like it."

"They do," I say.

He leans in. "You never know how it's going to go. Thumbs up, thumbs down. Where it's going to land on the Rotten Tomatoes Tomatoreader. The hype starts long before it releases. It was testing well but Ray's been worried about this for months 'cause it's an indie flick, I'm breaking out of the traditional hero role and tackling something a bit deeper. That, and we have new financiers. A privately-backed investment group."

"Just a little pressure," I say over the applause.

He nods. "It's a crazy business. Be glad you're not in it."

THERE'S A SMALL-ISH GATHERING AFTER THE SCREENING AT an old school Italian restaurant. The minute we walk in the door everyone notices Jake.

"Man of the hour," a guy says sidling up to him.

"Thanks," Jake says.

"Get ready for awards season," a woman says.

"You're too kind," he says.

"Jacob Jonathan Keller!" A woman hollers. "You, my darling, were fucking fabulous. Get over here."

I turn. Pinkie Stein and Ray Stark are seated at a table for eight in the corner. She flashes a toothy smile and waves. Ray still resembles a shark with less jagged teeth. Half the table's seats remain open.

"Have you met Pinkie Stein my publicist?" Jake takes my arm and guides me toward them. "Or Ray Stark, my agent?"

"Ray, yes. Pinkie, no."

"Ray's an asshole," he says. "Pinkie's a doll but don't get drunk with her. You'll end up hung over in Mexico drinking Bloody Mary's --"

"Getting massaged by half naked muscular men," I say, "Don't make me abandon the dream."

"Ha." His forehead crinkles as he laughs. "Nikki told you."

The crowd is bustling around us but time slows and suddenly it's just me and Jake. He's looking at me with mischief in his eyes. We're yards from Pinkie and Ray's table when he makes an abrupt detour from the table.

"Jake!" Ray hollers.

"Can't hear you," he says, and slides his hand down my arm, interlacing his fingers with mine. He leads out of the main dining room and down a narrow hallway.

"Where are we going?"

"Don't know," he says. "Keep moving. If we're lucky we can still escape."

🎕 11 🎕

BACKYARD FLOWER

BACKYARD FLOWER

WE PASS A BUSTLING GALLEY KITCHEN, STEAM RISING OFF sauce pans.

"Jake Keller," a man in a chef's uniform calls out.

Jake pauses. "Chef Massimo. Come va?"

They converse in Italian, Jake never letting go of my hand. The next thing I know, Massimo's placing small plates with multi-colored bow shaped pastas accented with real flowers on the counter. He gestures, explaining the samples in a mixture of Italian and English. "This," Massimo says, sprinkling a pinch of Parmesan on top, "is farfalle primavera made from flowers grown in the back yard."

The scent is heady, the farfalle arranged in the shape of a pinwheel. A large flower makes the hub on the white plates, the jewel-toned smaller flowers sprinkled on top of the pasta. The dish is so pretty, practically food porn obscene. "Edible flowers?" Jake asks.

"Purple chive blossoms," Massimo says.

Jake spears a farfalle and places it on my tongue. I close my mouth, then my eyes, my taste buds singing "Amazing Grace" because I suspect they might have died and gone to heaven.

"Grazie, Massimo," Jake says and tugs at my hand pulling me along with him. "We have to go. We're running late."

"We are?"

"Nah," he says. "I just want you to myself. Come on."

"Where are we going?"

"Where do you want to go, Evie?"

"Wherever you're going."

We come to a door marked in red letters "Open Only in Case of Emergency."

"We can't," I say. "It's not an emergency."

"It is for me," Jake says, and pushes it open. No alarms go off and we make our way into the night air. The door creaks shut, its hinges in need of a liberal dose of WD-40.

We look at each other and laugh. "Risk-taker," I say.

"You're my risk," he says. He walks me back against a concrete wall behind the restaurant and leans into me. He tilts my chin up and stares into my eyes. "Heal me, Evie."

"I'm trying, Jake."

He rakes his hand through my pixie cut and I flash to Dylan McAlister when he cut my waist-length locks because he thought it would ward off predators. But I am not here with Dylan, the guy I love who can't or won't put a ring on my finger.

I'm here with Jake Keller. He of the sweet eyes, and the bitter taint that consumes his soul. He's the man wooing me, the one who's treating me like I'm important.

He leans down and kisses me. He bites my lower lip then opens my mouth with his tongue. He runs his hand down my neck and my arm. Goosebumps erupt everywhere. The V between my legs throbs and I grow wet. "We should probably get back inside," I say. "They're expecting you."

"Let's not," he says, one hand traveling to the bottom of my skirt. He slips his hand underneath and lets his fingers travel along my thigh, touching, feeling, caressing. Shivers zip up and down my spine.

"We shouldn't be doing this," I say, aware of the muffled voices of the kitchen staff.

"Oh, we definitely should," he says. He traces his fingers over my sex. I clench my core and bite my lower lip. "Spread your legs for me, Evie."

I do as he asks.

"Better," he says. His deft fingers slip inside my panties, and find their way to my folds. He toys with my clit. I squirm under his touch and my breath comes quicker. "Someone could come out here," I say as he slips his other hand inside my dress and palms my breast. "Someone could take a picture."

"You said I was a risk taker." He rolls my nipple between his thumb and forefinger, and dips his head to my breast. He slips my dress down, and draws my nipple into his mouth – licking, nibbling, sucking.

He feels so good. I can't help it. I grind against his hand. He plays with my clit, strumming it faster and my breath comes in short, little gasps. "Inside me," I say.

"I thought we weren't supposed to be fooling around out here?" He returns his hand to my breast, and flicks my nipple between his fingers.

"Changed my mind." I say, arching into him. "Put your finger inside me."

He slips a finger inside me, then two, and I clench against him.

"I want to watch you come," he says, staring at me with those eyes. Those beautiful, Jake Keller eyes that make people go crazy. "I want to watch you come as I play with you outside this restaurant with all those pompous assholes inside eating beautiful food. Because I'm going to eat someone more beautiful and more delicious than they'll ever lay their mouths on tonight."

He drops to his knees, lifts my skirt with one hand and presses his mouth against my sex. His beard scrapes against the sensitive nub. He dips his tongue inside me as he goes down on me. Waves of pleasure course through me and I bite my lip as he savors me with his mouth. I cling to his muscular shoulder and steady myself.

"Come for me, Evie." He puts two fingers back inside me and I groan, arching into his hand as his thumb rubs against my clit.

I grind against his hand, moaning low under my breath until I lose all sense of time and space and come with two of his fingers inside me. "Oh, Jake. Oh!" I squeeze my eyes shut. Time stands still until I'm able to feel my arms and legs again.

"Beautiful." He pulls his fingers out, puts them in his mouth and sucks on them. "Delicious. Better than a backyard flower any day."

"You're bad," I say, slipping my dress back onto my shoulder. I slide my panties back up my legs, then smooth down my skirt. I reach for his zipper.

The back door to the restaurant flies open. "Jacob Jonathan Keller!" Pinkie Stein booms.

"What?" he says.

"Oh, Jesus Christ," she says. "Are you two out here fucking?"

"No, Pinkie," Jake says and grins.

"Whatever. People are waiting for you. Come on." She leaves.

"Sadly, even risk-takers have to return to business," Jake

says, adjusting himself. "Even sadder, the rest of this will have to wait."

"Bummer," I say.

"It's show business. Emphasis on the word 'business.'"

We walk back inside. The music is louder, the place more crowded than ten minutes ago.

Ray Stark pulls out a chair for me. "Nice to see you, Evelyn. I hope Jake saw fit to take you someplace important."

"Super important," Jake says.

Backed up against a garden wall with his tongue lavishing my sex has to count as super important.

Pinkie waves a hand, her large cocktail ring sparkling in the candlelight. "Nice to officially meet you, Evelyn. I'm Pinkie Stein. Let's order you a drink."

"Call me Evie," I say. "Seltzer, thanks."

"I thought the new investor was showing up tonight," Jake says sitting down next to me. "Did he make the screening?"

"Got there late," Ray says. "Hit traffic."

"Shocker," Jake says.

"Better late than never," Pinkie says.

"That's him," Ray says. "He just walked in the door."

"I'm confused," Pinkie says. "I thought he was Chinese."

I place my napkin on my lap and smooth it out.

"No," Ray says. "You heard me wrong. Easton Wolfe was coming back from a business trip to China."

Easton Wolfe? My skin prickles. Easton Wolfe? The boy we ran over in mom's car when I was thirteen-years-old? I break out in a sweat but don't look up. I am not about to look up.

MY BEST FRIEND

MY BEST FRIEND

"WHO'S THE GIRL WITH HIM?" PINKIE ASKS. "MRS. WOLFE? She's young, pretty."

My heart stops in my chest.

'Uh-oh,' Queasy says. *'Wasn't your pal Victoria in town to meet a client from China?'*

Good God, he's right. I shiver and glance up as my personal train wreck, Easton Wolfe, approaches the table. I can't see his date because she's behind him. Oh, God I hope it's not Victoria.

"I'm Easton Wolfe," he says. "Sorry we are late."

I scroll on my phone because I don't want to glance up at him. Out of the corner of my eye I see him extend his hand to Jake and they shake.

"I caught the last half of the movie," Easton says. "It looks terrific."

"Thanks," Jake says.

"Ray Stark," Ray says. "We've talked over the phone."

"Great to put a face to the name," Easton says.

"I'm Pinkie Stein."

"Terrific meeting you Pinkie."

I glance up, not wanting to look, but I need to. My shoulders are already creeping toward my ears.

"Since we're doing the introductions," Jake says, "this is Evelyn Berlinger. My consultant."

"Nice to see you again, Evelyn."

Easton's eyes are hard, just like the muscle ticking in his jaw. Just like the set of his lips as he glares at me. I could be frozen solid by Easton Wolfe's glare.

"I'd be remiss if I didn't introduce my date," he says as she turns toward us. "Amelia DeLadro."

Not Victoria. My best friend Amelia.

What remains of my breath transforms into puffs of chilly winter air escaping my mouth in shocked, short gasps.

"Evelyn." Amelia smiles. "Nice to meet you."

It's hard not to crawl out of my skin during the appetizers or the time that it takes everyone to finish their entrees. I wait a socially acceptable length of time and excuse myself.

"I'll join you," Amelia says.

We make our way to the restroom. "I thought you were in town for shopping," I say. "What are you doing here with Easton Wolfe?"

"Last minute thing," she says. "Madame Marchand got the call after I was already on a flight out here."

"Don't you remember I told you about him?"

"Of course, I remember," she says. "I thought all that was in the past. Do you two have something going on?"

"The last thing we had going on was two years ago when he kicked me out of his hotel in Vegas. He told me I wasn't allowed back into anything he owned."

"Shit. I wonder if that's why he called Ma Maison looking for a date for tonight?"

"What do you mean?"

"Photos of Jake Keller kissing you were on Instagram. They even got picked up by a few magazines. Maybe that threw him."

"What does that have to do with anything?"

The bathroom door squeaks and Pinkie walks in. "Having a party in here?"

"Yes," Amelia says.

"No," I say.

"Never throw a party in L.A. without inviting me," Pinkie says and heads into a stall. "I put the life in the party, ladies."

"Good to know." I tug on Amelia's sleeve. "See you back at the table," I call out to Pinkie.

As we head back to our table I say to Amelia, "What do you mean that's why Easton called Ma Maison? What do you mean the photos of Jake Keller threw him?"

"Maybe he saw them," she says. "Maybe he's still so angry at you. Maybe he's hot for you."

"Ugh, no. I used to be in love with his brother Wyatt. I was thirteen and he was my first love, but it was love none-the-less."

"I don't know, Evie. I bet those photos wound him up. He figured he'd see you tonight at Jake's gig, contacted Ma Maison, and put in a last minute request for a date."

We pass the kitchen with the steaming pots. An hour ago when I was here with Jake, the place smelled like food porn, but now it smells like Amelia's perfume, which for some reason never bothered me before tonight, but it does now.

"Whatever. Thanks for picking up the mail." I tap the letter in my purse. "That letter was from Fan."

"Get out," Amelia says. "What did he say?"

"It was weird. He mentioned the photo with Jake, too. He mentioned the box on my bed. Called it a 'gift.' You know what he didn't mention?"

"What?"

"He didn't mention breaking into my apartment."

"Why would he?" she asks. "He's not going to incriminate himself. Besides, maybe he *didn't* break in? Maybe he already had a key."

"No one has keys."

"Hazel O'Rourke has your keys. That's how I got your mail."

"Right," I say and chew on my lip.

"You gave me a key to your old place two years ago. I watered your plants when you were road tripping with Dylan McAlister. Remember?"

"Right," I say, wondering if I've missed something. Maybe someone really does have a key to my new place.

"You could have left your key for a workman, a delivery guy, your super," she says. She smiles at Easton as we approach the table.

"Right," I say. The smile she gives Easton feels like a paper cut. Thin, nearly invisible, and it stings.

"Or you gave it to the new person watering your plants when you left to go on a trip for one of these guys you're healing," she says.

"Right," I say. "I've got a question for you."

"What?"

"Are you going to sleep with Easton?"

"If he wants me to sleep with him? Yes."

The paper cuts multiply. Ten. Fifty."

"That going to be a problem?" She asks.

A hundred. I wonder if one can die from too many paper cuts. Jake smiles at me, leaning back in his chair.

It was so cold that day we ran over the Wolfe brothers. I'll never forget seeing them cross the path in front of our approaching car. The screech of tires. Punching Mom's arm because she was manic and texting and wouldn't stop. The sounds the boys made when we ran into them. I'll never forget walking past Easton, his seventeen-year-old body bloody and broken, lying on the side of the road on a cluster-fuck of a day.

Now Easton's eyes bore a cold hole through me. Goose-bumps raise on the backs of my arms as if anger has arrived in a gust of icy wind that threatens to snap fingers off my hands like frozen twigs.

"You're my BFF," Amelia says. "If you have a problem with me sleeping with Easton Wolfe you need to tell me now."

I felt so helpless when the paramedics hustled Easton into the back of that ambulance. Pain was painted all over his face, turning him into someone I almost didn't recognize.

I remember standing in the snow while the cops inter-viewed Mom and I tried to apologize to Easton for the unthinkable nightmare that had just gone down. He spat out, "Fuck you," and my soul shattered into a thousand pieces.

"I don't have a problem with you sleeping with Easton Wolfe." I lean closer to Amelia and whisper, "Do whatever you want with him."

JAKE KELLER LIES ON MY BED AND I STRADDLE HIM. I'M wearing a bra and thin, silk panties. He's shirtless, his six-pack abs contracting as he grinds his rock hard erection against my pelvis.

"Not yet," I say, and pull away. I stare into his delicious eyes and remind myself how lucky I am to be here. To be the person tasked with healing this sweet man.

His eyes have that glazed over look. "No one likes a tease," he says.

"No one likes an actor who doesn't campaign to win the big award."

"Point taken."

"Where do you go so late at night and come home even later?" I ask.

"Where do you think I go?"

"I don't know. The first night I was here in your house you came home drunk. The second time you knocked on my door you smelled of incense and were stone cold sober. The third time you just sat in that chair in your bungalow next to a stack of scripts. Want to tell me what's up?"

"You really want to know?"

"Yes."

"Fuck me first and I'll take you there you." He snags my panties with two fingers and slides them off. He unhooks my clasp and I shrug off my bra. He palms my tits, rubbing them, pulling me to him. He takes my nipple in his mouth, and sucks, while kneading my other breast. "So good," he says and slaps my ass. He hooks his hands on top of my pelvis and rolls on top of me.

I run a hand over his chest, enjoying the way his muscles ripple under my touch. "Take me there first," I say, "and then I'll fuck you after."

He kisses me on the lips then lifts my hands over my head. He pins my wrists to the mattress with one hand and lines up his hard, beautiful cock against the V between my legs. He rubs it against my clit until I squirm and moan.

"Changed my mind," I say. "We should definitely have sex first."

86

"Maybe," he says, "And maybe not."

"Oh come on. Now who's the tease?" I arch my pelvis. He'd have to be a eunuch not to want to be inside me right now.

"So demanding," he says, and pushes his beautiful cock inside me. I shiver. He feels so good. He kisses me on my lips as he rocks into me slowly at first, then harder. I close my eyes and enjoy the Jake Keller ride.

We come.

Me first with him inside me, his fingers playing with my clit, my legs on his shoulders. A minute later he explodes. He closes his eyes and bites his fleshy lower lip. He thrusts into me harder and harder. I feel him deep in my center.

He collapses on top of me and I wrap my arms around him, rubbing his shoulders, caressing his back.

"Wow," he says.

"Wow," I say. "Rise and shine. Time to show me where you sneak away to at night."

❧ 13 ❧

CROWN OF THORNS

CROWN OF THORNS

———

HALF AN HOUR LATER, JAKE PARKS HIS MOTORCYCLE IN THE lot across from a Spanish-style church in front of mountainous foothills. We make our way toward St. Agnes Basilica.

"Is this your church?" I ask.

"I haven't belonged to a church in decades," he says, and holds out his hand.

I take it and we follow the Spanish pavers punctuating the scrubby short grass to the entrance.

"Except for filming the movie, I hadn't even stepped inside a real church until I came here with Nikki six months ago," he says.

"Is this Nikki's church?"

"I have no idea. Nikki came here for a Women in Film talk that I was giving with one of her friends."

We walk past gnarled old rose bushes. A worn statue of St. Agnes stands outside the steps leading to the church's

88

vestibule. Agnes looks kind-hearted. She reminds me a little of Nikki.

It's surprisingly airy inside the sanctuary with its arched ceilings. Gilded paintings of saints in jewel tones line the walls. Jake pauses at the font, dips his fingers in the holy water, and crosses himself. I follow suit.

"You're Catholic?" he asks.

"Raised," I say. "I don't practice much anymore but it's in my blood."

"Me too. I left in high school." He walks up a side aisle and takes a seat midway from the front. An older priest is conducting a late afternoon mass, a modest number of parishioners gathered in the front of the church. Jake pats the seat open next to him.

I sit. "The art in this church is gorgeous."

"My new movie has a scene about the crown of thorns story," Jake says. "The painting of the crown being pressed onto Jesus's head weirds me out."

"Why?" I ask as telltale goosebumps erupt on the backs of my arms.

"If you set aside the faith part Jesus of Nazareth's story is pretty epic. Similar to Gandhi, Martin Luther King Jr., he was a peaceful rebel. He bucked the system and suffered the ultimate punishment."

"I'll say."

"His captors crushed that crown of thorns into his skull right before he was crucified to taunt him. 'Oh, so you're a Prince? The Son of God? Here's your crown, dude. Who's a prince, now?'"

'*This is dark,*' Queasy says, wiggling his hairy toes deep into my stomach.

'*Maybe you should talk about this over a glass of wine back at Jake's house.*' Hope says.

"I'm the last person to suffer a God complex," Jake

continues, "but sometimes I feel that scorn, you know? 'Oh, you're Jake Keller, the movie star? The guy who stars in all the popcorn carjack movies with the stupid plots. Not a real actor. You suck and your acting sucks too.'"

"People can be assholes," I say. My head hurts.

"I want them to believe the words I say. I want them to take me seriously. I need my words to be taken seriously." Jake points to the sanctuary at the front of the church. "See that painting?"

"Yes." Pain throbs harsher behind my left eye and I wince.

"Jesus bears the cross on his shoulders on his way to be crucified. He knows they're making him haul the instrument of his execution. He knows they were dicking him around in this of all moments. And then he stumbles. Did he know he'd get back up? Or did he wonder if he should just lay on the dirt and let them end it there?"

'Ground yourself,' Hope says.

I pinch the thick web of flesh between my thumb and forefinger, searching for the sharpness of that acupuncture spot to stop me from slipping into a full-blown empathic reaction. But Jake's burden lies heavy on my shoulders and I am already crumpling inside from its weight. My breath comes quicker, more shallow.

'Pinch harder,' Queasy says. *'Stomp your feet. Shake your fingers. Get a grip.'*

'She's inside his wound,' Hope says. *'She can identify it. Diagnose it.'*

I grit my teeth. Jake's injury is dull and heavy. The anguish, heavy like a mantle on my shoulders, spreads to my throat. It's thick with bottled-up guilt and unspoken words. Confusion creeps into my brain like a cancer that has metastasized. The cross that Jake bears is almost too much. His sadness makes me want to scream. He carries his own version of the weight of the world and it's too much. I fear I can't help him.

"And yet Jesus gets up and moves forward," Jake says. "Through the pain, through the unfairness, through the shittiness of his messed up situation. He was targeted and taken out because of politics. His arrest was a thuggish power play. And yet he bears that damn cross, moves on, and just gets it done. I don't think I'd be able to do that. I don't think I'd have the grace or the dignity or the strength."

The depression deep in my shoulders will squat there for a few hours. I'll become smaller on the inside, and let his cross take the outer circle of my being while I occupy the inner circle. We'll cohabitate like roommates who politely despise each other. Eventually his crucifix will realize I'm not the person that needs to be nailed to it. Eventually it will relinquish its nails and leave.

The priest is giving communion to the handful of parishioners gathered in the front. "The body of Christ," he says, placing a wafer on a women's tongue.

"You want to take Communion?" I ask Jake.

"I don't do that anymore," he says.

"Why not?"

"It never worked out all that well for me in the past."

❧ 14 ❧

KILLING TIME

KILLING TIME

———

I SIT ACROSS FROM ADAM ON A LOW SETTEE AT HENRI'S boutique department store waiting for Jake to finish up his alterations. "I'm kind of surprised the tailor doesn't come to him," I say.

"Salvatore normally does," Adam says. "But he's out of the country."

Ping-ping-ping.

I check my texts.

> **Mom:** *When are you coming home?*

I sigh.

Evie: *I'm at work.*

> **Mom:** *You're always at work.*

Evie: *Someone has to pay the bills.*

Mom: *I can leave this place you know. I can get a little studio apartment in the city.*

Mom*: Close to you.*

Mom: *Or Ruby.*

Mom*: To be honest with you, I'm not really sure how much good this place is doing for me anymore.*

I frown.

Evie: *Don't say that.*

Evie: *You've been doing great.*

Mom: *I don't feel so great.*

Evie: *Are you taking your meds?*

Mom: *Yes.*

Evie: *Are you sure?*

Mom: *Yes.*

Evie*: Do you have pain anywhere?*

Evie: *Like back pain. Stomach pain. Heart pain?*

Mom: *Not really.*

Evie: Did you talk to the doctor or nurses about this?

Mom: Yes. Kind of. Not really.

I tap my shoe on the plush carpet embroidered with Henri's gold and crimson logo.

Evie: Which is it, Mom?

Evie: You either talked to the docs and caretakers at the Institute or you didn't.

Evie: Yes or no?

Mom: I don't know!

Evie: Why don't I call you later today?

Mom: Fine. Call whenever you want.

Mom: I'll hold my breath.

Evie: Work with me on this, please.

Mom: Fine. I've got nothing else to do.

Mom: Just hanging around.

Mom: Waiting for my busy, talented daughters to visit me.

Evie: Call you later.

Evie: Promise.

"Rrr," I say and shove the phone in my purse.

"A mom text?" Adam asks.

"Yes." I say.

"I know the exasperated tone well," he says. "I think it's universal."

Jake walks out of the dressing room dressed in charcoal pants, a fitted T-shirt and a casual, cashmere jacket. "What do you think?"

"Hot," Adam says. "If you weren't my best friend I'd bang you."

"The tailor checked my file. He said I gained five pounds," Jake says.

"The potato chips," I say. "Still hot. I'd bang you too."

Jake cracks a smile in my direction. "Yes, please. I thought you'd never ask."

"Yeah, yeah, get a room." Adam grabs his phone from his pocket and walks away from the dressing room into the thick of the menswear department. "We've got a meeting with Howard from Tru Blue. We can't be late."

"This casual, but stunning ensemble works for the premiere right?" Jake asks, striking an affected pose. "The critics usually say I dress like a hobo."

"You look good to me," I say, smiling.

"Do you want to check it out thoroughly? You know, in the dressing room?" He pulls me to him. His dick is waking up, insistent, throbbing, against my pelvis.

Lust rises in me and whispers dirty things in my ear. Goosebumps erupt on the backs of my arms. "Tempting."

He kisses me, and places his hand on my neck, gradually making his way down to my shoulder before landing on the small of my back. This man is making me wet in the men's department of an upscale Beverly Hills department store, which is a first for me. "But you've got a meeting, right?"

"Screw the meeting," he says, nuzzling my ear. "I'd rather screw you."

"Damn it." Adam says. "Tru Blue's pushed back the meeting a couple of hours. No reason to go back home. We'd just have to turn around and come back. Hey... I've got an idea. A way to kill time." He waggles his eyebrows suggestively.

"Nope," I say. "Not up for that."

"Me either," Jake says.

"Stop it, you freakazoid sex-crazed weirdos," Adam says. "That's the last thing I want to do with you two. Come with me."

15

VENICE BEACH BOARDWALK

VENICE BEACH BOARDWALK

"THAT'S THE DRESS," JAKE SAYS, WATCHING ME CHECK IT out in the full length mirror at Henri's Evening Dress department. "Elegant. Pretty."

"I'd fuck you in that dress," Adam says.

"No," Jake says. "You will not."

"I just mean... never mind," Adam says.

It fits me perfectly. The fabric is a shimmery silk concoction with metallic threads. I could almost pass for one of those golden statues they give out at the movie and TV awards.

"Let's put it on my tab and blow out of here. I've got better things to do," Jake says with a knowing smirk.

VICTORIA, AMELIA, AND I WALK DOWN THE TRIPLE WIDE

sidewalk on Venice Beach Boardwalk, an assortment of languages, and weed wafting through the air. A string of weathered hole-in-the-wall buildings house eateries, tattoo parlors, and T-shirt shops. To our right is the Pacific Ocean, a wide swath of sand interspersed with a skateboard park, outdoor showers, a court lined with basketball hoops and painted circles.

"You guys are having all the fun," Victoria says, stripping off her Chicago Bears T-shirt, and shoving it in a bag with her other purchases. She shrugs on her new Venice Beach Lifeguard T-shirt. "I'm doing all the grunt work."

"How so?" I ask.

"You're going to the Hollywood parties. I'm beating a middle-aged man with a riding crop as he crawls across the floor with a gag in his mouth."

"You're the one who picked kink as your specialty," Amelia says.

"You told me to do that," she says.

"I did, didn't I? Oops, sorry. Well, you know, specialties help you brand."

We wander over to the basketball courts. They players are all ages, moving fast and furious. I can't help but wonder if a future NBA star is working on his game right here.

"Easton's a producer on Jake Keller's movie," Amelia says. "We're going to the screening tonight. I bet between me and Evie we can score you tickets."

"Really?" Victoria asks.

"Yes," I say feeling irritated, not knowing why.

"That would be amazing," Victoria says. "A much needed break. Hey – not to be judgmental, but there are some cray cray people on this boardwalk."

"The guy in the Michael Jackson mirror costume scares me," Amelia says.

"Speaking of weirdos," Victoria says. "Did you send the fan letter to the cops?"

"Yes," I say. We wander back toward the boardwalk and I spot a cute taco truck. "I'm hungry."

We grab Mexican food, sit on the sand and munch on ceviche, tacos, and quesadillas. "I sent the detectives pictures. I'll give the actual letter to them when I get home," I say. "They didn't make it sound like an emergency."

"Do they have any leads on who left that box?" Victoria asks.

"Not that I know."

"What was in it?" Amelia wipes hot sauce from her lips.

"Hair," Victoria says.

"Ew," Amelia says.

"It was the night before I left for this gig. It's not a big deal, really."

"You were crawling out of your skin," Victoria says. "I've never seen you that upset."

"So creepy," Amelia says. "Do you think it's the guy from a few years back?"

I shrug. "I don't know."

"What if – oh, never mind," she says.

"What?" I ask.

"What if it's from a client?"

"Why would one of her clients do that?" Victoria asks.

"I don't know," Amelia says. "I used to get fan letters. One person even tracked me down."

"Get out," Victoria says.

"Suzie Sandowski from high school. She found out I work for Ma Maison."

"Was that awkward?" I ask.

"Kind of. She thought my life was exciting. She wanted to write a book about me."

"Seriously?" Victoria asks.

"She writes true crime. I told her I'm not a criminal."

"You're probably more noteworthy than anyone else she went to high school with," I say.

"Which does not necessarily a book make,'" Amelia says. "I just want to make a decent living and enjoy this crazy job while I can. Someday, I'll leave this behind and carve out a normal life."

"What's a normal life?" Victoria asks.

"The happily ever after," Amelia says, a faraway look drifting across her face. "Mr. Right. He'll be devoted with a decent job. He doesn't have to be exciting. He can be an accountant or an attorney or a banker. Someone who pays the bills, worships the ground I walk on, and wants two kids. If he already has kids I'll happily be a stepmom."

My heart lurches because in this moment Amelia once again resembles the grade school teacher she used to be: her arm nestled around a crying five-year-old. Sweet. Earnest. Like when I first met her at St. Matthew's Elementary School.

"It'll happen," Victoria says.

"It will totally happen," I say. Amelia's a sweetheart, a total catch. I want her to find the fairytale ending. I want her to find that guy.

THE MOVIE PREMIERE'S FIVE DAYS AWAY AND WE ATTEND another screening of Jake's movie at a retro-style theatre on Hollywood Boulevard.

After the applause, and the obligatory well wishers who stop by to congratulate Jake on his performance, he runs a finger up and down my arm and gives me one of his panty melting smiles.

Ray Stark stands on the opposite side of the aisle, and eyes me with one of his signature creepy looks.

"Let's skip the after party," Jake says. "Let's go home. I think the guys went bowling tonight and took Nikki with them. We'd have the entire house to ourselves. Just think of all the trouble we could get into."

"Tempting, but no. You're the man of the hour," I say. "Everyone wants to talk to you at the party. Besides, Ray is giving me dagger eyes. He'll shred me to bits with his jagged little shark teeth if I don't get you up and running in time for awards season. He'll have my hide."

"I'll have your hide," Jake says, nuzzling his face into my neck. The scruff of his beard makes all the little hairs on the backs of my arms stand up. "And trust me – it'll be more fun than what Ray Stark could do any day."

"I don't doubt that," I say. "But you're not paying me for that. You're paying me to help you heal."

WE TAKE MULHOLLAND DRIVE TO THE AFTER PARTY. IT'S A windy two lane road on top of the Santa Monica Mountains that straddles the busy Westside to the right and the colossal Valley region on the left.

The driver pulls up to an estate and a guard waves us through the gates.

Jake and I make our way toward the main house, its doors wide open. The sound of a Frank Sinatra song greets us. A breeze kicks up the night air, rustling the leaves on eucalyptus trees. Wind chimes hanging from the wooden eaves tinkle.

We walk inside a house already packed with people. Floor to ceiling windows line one wall of the sunken living room, and millions of lights from the Valley sparkle below us.

I spot Victoria on the far side of the room with a hand-some middle-aged guy I recognize from some magazine or newspaper – I can't keep up. She mouths 'Thank you', squeezes his arm, and propels him into another room.

I glance over at the bar. Easton has one arm wrapped around Amelia's waist. Ray stands next to the white-brick fireplace with a couple of guys who look like younger versions of him. Hungry baby sharks with jagged baby shark teeth.

"Jake," Ray beckons.

"Go," I say. "Make Ray happy."

"We're staying for ten minutes." Jake kisses me. "Then we're blowing out of here."

"Sounds good," I say.

He turns to walk away but pauses. "You ever think about sticking around L.A. for a bit longer than what was originally planned?"

I gaze up at my beautiful movie star. He is stunning. A thick head of hair. Full lips. There is a sweetness to this man that no matter what he's been through has not been stamped out.

I fantasize for a moment about how great it would feel to run away with him. To escape from the crowds that want everything. "We can talk about the future when we've accomplished what I came here to do in the first place," I say.

"Okay, boss." He smiles and walks into the crowd. They suck him in and within twenty seconds I can barely see the top of his head. He's consumed by a sea of people clambering for his attention.

Sticking around here for a bit longer isn't going to happen. I'm here to get Jake back up and running. Let the Hollywood machine have its way with him. I'll help him campaign for the award I know he so richly deserves, and then I'll leave. He'll get on with his life and I'll get on with mine and I will forever remember the time we had together.

I pinch the acupuncture spot on the thick web of flesh that lies between my thumb and forefinger, and this time its sharpness grounds me.

I glance back at the bar. Easton looks up at me, his eyes practically pinning me to the wall. The room goes from warm to cold in the blink of an eye, goose bumps spread across the backs of my arms.

I break free from his gaze and wander outside, pumping my hands into fists to get the blood flow going again.

16

BLESS YOUR HEART

BLESS YOUR HEART

I GRAB A BURGER, SALAD, AND A BEER FROM THE BUFFET table, and sit down next to Adam at a fire pit in the far corner of the property. It's summer, but still a chilly night.

"How's our guy doing?" Adam cranes his neck and glances back at the house.

"I don't know." I turn and peer at Jake who's talking with a group of people including Ray.

"I think he's doing better," Adam says. "I know you told me you don't sleep with all your clients but whatever you're doing with Jake is working."

"I haven't done anything yet."

"He looks happier. He's taking meetings, he's open to new projects. It's a start."

"You said you grew up together. What was that like?"

"Small town outside of Albuquerque. It was dusty. Low maintenance. We lived down the street from each other. Our folks were working a lot so we suffered from benign neglect. No helicopter parenting for us."

"So, what'd you do?" Out of the corner of my eye I see that Amelia's left Easton's side and is chatting with a few folks that I recognize from a Reality TV show. She's laughing. Maybe her happily-ever-after lies in L.A. rather than Chicago.

"We took off on our bikes, and rode wherever we wanted. We climbed hills, played ball, snuck into places we weren't supposed to sneak into," he says.

"Sounds somewhat idyllic."

"It wasn't half bad," he says. "Oh, and there was church. A lot of Catholic church. Catholic grade school. High school. Altar boys. When we weren't being dumb wild boys we were making up for our sins in church. Until the shit hit the fan."

"What do you mean?"

"The scandal with the priest. Father Tate. Ugh. What a nightmare that turned into."

"What happened?"

"What do you think happened?" Adam asks. "A bad priest. A bunch of kids. I was one of them."

"I'm so sorry," I say. "How do you get over something that horrible?"

"Years and years of therapy," he says. "And I talk about it now. Being silent only gives it more power."

Easton comes and sits down in the chair next to me. He crosses his legs, his hard quad muscles tensing under his pants.

Adam turns to Easton. "So? The movie. What do you think?"

"People are loving it," Easton says. "It seems like they're accepting Jake in a grittier role not just his standard action adventure romance fare."

"Which means he'll be taken more seriously," Adam says, "and get offered the juicier parts."

"It's a win-win for everyone," Easton says. He turns to me. "What do you think?"

"I don't know that much about movies – but as far as I can tell – I think it's all coming along pretty well," I say, a little shocked Easton was gracious enough to ask my opinion.

"Good. I've been meaning to ask. Does it bother you I hired Amelia to be my date for the movie launch?"

"And, I'm out of here." Adam springs out of his chair looking like someone lit a fire under his ass. "I never dish on the 'who's dating who' talk. Dangerous! Have an amazing night. Bye."

"Bye," I say, wishing that he'd stay.

"Amelia's a sweet girl." Easton drinks from a frosty long neck. "I didn't know you two were best friends when I picked her."

It bugs me that Easton's sexy. It irritates me that he smells crisp and intoxicating, like the scent of a brilliantly colored forest on a perfect autumn day.

I kick off my shoes, and the crackling logs warm the bottoms of my bare feet. "I don't care," I lie.

"Good," he says. "I was starting to sweat it."

"Bless your heart, Easton. Keep Amelia around." I move my chair away from his. "Date her. Marry her. Have a kid with her."

"I haven't quite gone there," he says.

"I don't care if you do, because at the end of the day that's what she wants. Just *please*, Easton —be nice to Amelia. If you knowingly hurt her – as God is my witness – I'll hurt you back."

"Slow down, Liam Neeson in every action movie ever," he says, adjusting his chair to face mine. "You're over-reacting. The thing with me and Amelia is just a gig."

"*I'm* over-reacting?" My fingers curl into a fist.

'Do not punch that man,' Hope says. *'Use your energy productively.'*

'Punch that asshole,' Queasy says. *'You'll never ever feel that good again.'*

I squeeze my nails into my palm until they bite. "You're the guy who called Ma Maison and hired my friend to accompany you for a week of Hollywood debauchery just so you could – oh, I don't know – one up me? One up Jake?"

"Not Jake," Easton says, shaking his head.

"Me? You're going to all this effort to for me? You're wasting your money."

"No." He shakes his head. "Hiring Amelia is just research."

"Research, right." *Ugh, I hate this man.* "Research for what? Will you be funding pornos in the future?"

"Ha. You're funny. I didn't expect you to have a sense of humor."

"Yeah, life knocked most of that out of me." I take a swig of my beer, and stare into the flames because I need to focus on something and I refuse to look into Easton's eyes because his gaze burns hotter than any fire ever could. "I can't believe you're related to Wyatt."

"Do you even remember my brother?"

"I'll never forget your brother," I say, my heart thumping in my chest, my face flushing with warm, pissed-off, angry blood. He's pushing all my buttons and I need to get a grip. I'm not here for Easton Arrogant Wolfe. "Wyatt was the nicest, kindest boy in the world."

"What do you really know about Wyatt, sweetheart? As far as I can tell you haven't talked with him in thirteen years. You and your mom weren't exactly pounding down our door with apologies after the accident."

"You don't know the half of it," I say, my palm itching, dying to punch him. "You don't know..."

"What? Don't know that your mom served time?" He asks. "I know."

"That was a just and fair sentence." I grind my teeth. "Mom was committed to making amends. It was part of her penance."

"But not so easy for you, I imagine." He scoots his chair closer to mine. His dirty blond hair falls behind his ears, and down the nape of his neck. His T-shirt skims the hard planes of his muscular chest. "Tell me, Evie. Did you heal Jake Keller yet?"

"What are you talking about?" The skin on my throat and chest flush hotter.

"You know exactly what I'm talking about."

I know the word is out about what I do. But now the word is out with a guy I despise and it's awkward bordering on painful. "It's not for me to share," I say.

"Dylan McAlister told me what you did for him."

'Goddamn Dylan and his talky mouth,' Queasy says.

'Dylan likes to help people,' Hope says.

"Did what?" I ask, playing dumb.

"You know. McAlister told me how you helped him get his game back."

"Take what he says with a grain of salt," I say, thoroughly irritated with Dylan right now. "We have a relationship. It's complicated."

"Complicated. Right. Martin Gunter Research Scientist Nerd was complicated. But you know that." He rakes his gaze over me. It lands on my lips as if he is willing me to take the bait.

I know exactly who he's talking about but I'm not going to answer him.

"Martin Gunter was inches away from cracking a genetic breakthrough for kids with Pitt Hopkins when he shut down. He couldn't work, couldn't concentrate, was missing deadlines," Easton says. "He lay in bed for days on end watching *The Great British Bake Off*. He was driving me nuts. Then he goes and hires you."

"I can't talk about that."

"I can. Martin told me he hired Evelyn Berlinger, a 21st century courtesan out of Ma Maison in Chicago. My ears pricked up. *Ding, ding, ding* – I'm hearing about Evelyn Berlinger again. First it was Dylan. Then it was Martin. Apparently, little Evelyn is all grown up, working as an escort at Ma Maison and she's healing broken men. Weird. It's not all that different from the way you tried to keep Wyatt alive after the accident."

"You don't know that," I say. How in the hell could he know what I was doing with Wyatt after the accident? Easton was lying twisted and broken in a snow bank when I walked past him.

Amelia looks over at us from across the yard and cocks her head. 'You okay?' she mouths.

I nod curtly.

"I do know that," Easton says. "You figured out what was shutting Martin down. You helped him deal with the shitty thing eating away at him. You got him up and running and back to the lab. He cracked that piece of the code and now, God willing after a ton of testing, we'll have drug studies we can use with those kids that would never have stood a chance a few years back."

"I can't talk about that."

"Three guys shared how you helped them heal, Evelyn. I'm impressed with your work, but don't you think it's ironic that you're healing people for a living when you and your mother broke me and my brother thirteen years ago?"

I rake a hand through my hair.

Anger rolls off Easton in jagged waves.

Amelia strides across the lawn toward us.

I stand up and slip on my shoes because I'm getting as far away from this guy as my legs can carry me.

"Leaving already?" Easton asks.

"Yes." Amelia can fuck him. She can suck his cock. She can roll around in all his stack of credit cards and money and whatever else it is he's buying her. I am thanking God it is Amelia or Victoria or anyone else in the world who has to deal with this man. As long as it's not me.

"Why don't you hold onto what happened thirteen years ago for the rest of your life, Easton," I say. "Why don't you hold onto it tight, like a lover? Even better, carve it into your skin."

"It's already carved into my skin," Easton says. "I have a scar that goes from my hip to my thigh from where the bone was fractured, and splintered pieces punctured the muscles. It took three surgeries to put my leg back together."

I cringe.

Amelia approaches. "Hey, what's up?"

"I'm sorry," I say to Easton as my heart twists in my chest. "Maybe the accident wasn't completely my fault. I wasn't behind the wheel. I wasn't driving the car, you know."

Amelia places a hand on Easton's shoulder. She's wearing a new diamond tennis bracelet. "Gorgeous place, isn't it?" she asks. "Everyone tells me the Valley's a little rougher to live in than the Westside. But if this is roughing it the Valley, count me in."

"Count me out," I say and make my way toward the house. Toward Jake Keller. Toward my job and far, far away from my past.

"I'm sorry if I was rude, Evie," Easton calls after me.

"It's Evelyn," I call back. "You can call me Evelyn."

17

WATCHING THE CHILDREN

WATCHING THE CHILDREN

VICTORIA'S GIG WITH THE SUBMISSIVE BUSINESSMAN IS OVER and she's flying back to Chicago this afternoon. I meet her for an early bite at a hole-in-the wall diner on Pico Boulevard. Autographed 8 X 10 pictures of Hollywood B and C list actors line the interior like wallpaper. I spot Nikki's headshot high in a corner. She looks younger, lighter, hopeful.

"Did you crack open the mysterious Jake Keller yet?" Victoria asks, smearing cream cheese on a bagel.

"Not yet."

"I saw him last night at the party. He didn't look completely disengaged. You must be doing something right."

"I hope so. But whatever's working him feels complicated."

"That means you're getting close," she says. "You know what they say. It's always darkest before the dawn."

"Yeah, well this dawn has heavy baggage in tow. I haven't identified the belief that's messing him up."

"You will," she says, downing her coffee and signaling the waitress. "I talked to Amelia last night. She's having a great time out here."

"Good for her."

"Are you thinking about telling her that your story with Easton Wolfe isn't over yet?"

I choke on my eggs. "What are you talking about?"

"Honey," she says. "I saw you two angry eye fucking each other."

I swipe a napkin across my mouth. "Easton and I were not angry eye fucking each other."

"And I am a Princess of Nigeria and will give you one *million* dollars if you help transfer my money into a US bank."

"Stop," I say.

"You're lying to yourself."

"Am not. There's nothing between me and Easton. Besides, my focus is on Jake Keller."

"As it should be."

WE STAND ON THE SIDEWALK AND PEER INTO THE WINDOW of a thrift shop filled with gently used treasures as we wait for Victoria's ride. "What are you going to do when you get back to Chicago?" I ask.

"Get a salt scrub and a two hour massage. Dominating men isn't the easiest of jobs. I think I'm getting a repetitive motion injury in my shoulder. Maybe I should file for Workmen's Comp."

"I don't think Ma Maison covers that."

"Nonetheless I'm marching down there when I get back. I'm wrestling Madame Marchand to the ground and I'm going to make her tell me what's going on with the change of ownership."

"The ownership change worries me," I say. "You?"

"Same."

"Is it even happening? We heard about it a few times and then Madame goes def con silent."

"Oh, it's happening," Victoria says. "Next few weeks I think."

"I hope they don't let people go."

"Management doesn't care about us." She waves her arms at a green hatchback and it pulls over. "All bets are off."

"I hate change. Update me if you hear anything?"

"Will do," she says. Her ride pulls away from the curb. She rolls down the window and sticks her head out "Good luck cracking open Movie Star."

"Thanks."

"For what it's worth?"

"Yeah?"

"Do yourself a favor and fuck Easton Wolfe for real."

I flip her the bird.

She blows me a kiss.

———

IT'S THE MORNING OF THE PREMIERE. I STEP INTO THE foyer at Jake's house, the sun streaming through the windows. It's as though even the weather knows this is supposed to be a happy day.

The adrenaline's flowing at Casa de Keller. Rock and roll blares from the jukebox. The house is a hub of activity, the people that make Jake's domestic life run like clockwork moving and grooving because they too are fired up. One of the guys from Jake's crew passes me in the hallway carrying several Henri's garment bags. "Happy Tuesday. Where do you want these?"

"Happy Tuesday," I say. "Upstairs in the bedrooms, thank you."

Brandt answers the door, fielding a delivery of an enormous flower arrangement. He juggles gift baskets and a bottle of Champagne.

"I'll help."

"Perfect," he says, and walks toward the kitchen.

I grab a few boxes and follow him in.

"Everything goes on the table," Nikki says, directing the flow like she's done this before.

I set down the box. "Morning." I walk to the fridge and make myself a bowl of yogurt with fresh fruit and granola. The gifts are piling up on the kitchen table. "This is better than Christmas."

"You have no idea how much money goes into properly sucking up," Nikki says, shuffling baskets around, trying to make room for more. "This gift box alone probably has five hundred dollars worth of stuff. Organic chocolate from the Netherlands. Natural bath salts from Peru. Wine from Argentina."

"There's ten of those baskets on the table," I say. A mishmash of envelopes is piling up on the corner of the table. "Who sends all the cards?"

"Well wishes inked inside by folks who want to stay on Jake's radar."

"What does he do with all of this?"

"He gives most of it away. His crew gets first dibs."

I hold out my hand. "I'll take the Netherlands chocolate bar, please."

"Yours," she says, passing it to me.

I peel back the wrapper and sink my teeth into the chocolate, my taste buds falling into an orgasmic coma. "Holy moly, what do they put in this stuff?"

Nikki holds up a letter and squints. "This envelope's addressed to you. 'Miss Evelyn Berlinger' care of Jake Keller, care of Ray Stark's Management Company. That's weird."

I stop chewing.

'Oh, Evie,' Hope says. *'Not today.'*

'Crap.' Queasy stretches in my gut. *'Here we go again.'*

"How is this possible?" I ask, feeling a little lightheaded.

"Someone knows you're staying with Jake but doesn't know his address. They probably looked up the name and address of his management online," she says and hands me the envelope.

"Thanks." I wander outside, clutching the chocolate bar and the letter. I take a seat on a chaise next to the pool and open it up, my hands already shaking. Maybe it's nothing. Maybe Hazel O'Rourke, my neighbor in Chicago, wants Jake's autograph.

But it's not from Hazel.

Dear Evelyn:

Have you ever noticed that most folks are so busy with the drama playing out in their own lives to look in front of them?

Example. Busy mom or dad takes their kids to the library. It's a fun outing. The kids wander around the book stacks. They run their hands over them, pick them up, flip through the pages, hear the flutter.

Mom sees a flier for 'Story Time' at the library when she's

checking the books out at the front desk. It might be a nice experience for little Ashley and Josh and give her an hour break so she can catch up on some of her busy work.

"Hey," Jake says walking across the lawn. "Shouldn't you be getting ready?"

"In a minute," I say, and keep reading.

Does Mom notice the guy who sits at a table too close to the children's section? Does she see the same guy seated once again too close to the children's section the next time she brings the kids to Story Time?

Does anyone notice this guy isn't really here for the stories?

He's here watching the children.

One day Ashley goes missing. Mom and Dad are out of their minds with worry. The cops trace back all the routines, all the patterns until they stumble upon the guy at the library who sat too close to the children's section during Story Time.

I know you were upset that I left the box on your bed but I also know you're smart. You had to understand that gift's symbolism.

A jewelry box.

How many times have you been gifted jewelry since you started this consulting job? More than a dozen? Less than a hundred? Hair – well that should be obvious. A covering – do I even have to explain that part?

I grow weary of explaining all this to you.

Jake sits down next to me and kisses my neck. "The hair and makeup person's arrived. Deal with whatever this is, later."

"In a moment," I say and keep reading, my muscles tensing.

Do you think corporate consulting job is the right job for you? Maybe you should think about giving up this line of work. Maybe you should think about going home. Maybe your family needs you.

I only want what's best for you, Evelyn.

I am, as always,

Your Devoted Fan

I drop the letter onto the grass and I must have dropped my breath along with it because suddenly I can't breathe.

Jake picks up the letter. "What's going on?"

"I don't know." My hand flies to my chest and if I press it hard enough I might be able to find breath somewhere within me. I might be able to inhale and exhale again. I glance around at the house, the pool, the eco-friendly landscaped yard with the pretty flowers. It's all so beautiful and yet all the fame and money in the world can't buy you peace of mind if somebody's stalking you. All of a sudden I'm crying.

Jake springs to his feet, coiled and angry. "What kind of sick bastard would write something like this to you?"

"I don't know." I wipe away tears. I've never seen an angry Jake Keller. He is formidable.

"Probably some asshole who's jealous you're with me and not him. I'm going to get Ray and his people on this."

"It's not the first letter," I say. "This happened a few years ago. It happened before I flew out here to see you. I need to give this back to the cops back in Chicago."

"Oh, Evie." He reluctantly passes it back to me. He pulls me against his strong, secure chest, and into his sheltering arms. His kindness. His sweetness. "I'm so sorry."

✿ 18 ✿

BREAK A LEG

BREAK A LEG

IN MY ROOM, GLYNNIS THE MAKEUP LADY – A MIDDLE-AGED woman who with blue hair, lip piercings and tattoos who looks fiercer than I'll ever be – applies finishing touches to my face while Nikki watches.

"Look up," she says. I tilt my head and Glynnis brushes bronzer under my jaw, then down my cleavage.

"You look great," Nikki says.

"Thanks," I say, slide a bill from my purse and tip the makeup lady.

"Thanks doll. Have fun tonight." She grabs her kit and leaves.

"I'm sorry about the letters," Nikki says. "That's so creepy."

"You don't know the half of it. The cops back in Chicago are handling it."

"Can you compartmentalize this? Ignore it for tonight?

It's an indie film with an indie budget, but your first premiere is always special."

"Good idea," I say.

"Have fun. And turn off your phone."

"An even better idea."

A FEW COP CARS ARE PARKED ON THE STREETS OF Westwood. Bleachers are set up on the sidelines sequestering cheering fans. A red carpet stretches down the block cordoned off by velvet ropes. Security guards dressed in black T-shirts and pants wearing sunglasses and earpieces are stationed every twenty feet all the way to the theatre's entrance.

Nikki pulls the Range Rover up to the entrance and slips the car in park. Jake looks at me. "Ready?"

I apply a coat of lipstick. "Yes."

"You look gorgeous," Jake says. "How are you feeling?"

"I'm okay." I hear the fans hollering from outside the limo. Flashbulbs are already popping. "I'm good."

"Sure?" he asks.

"Yup."

"Are you ready, boss?" Nikki asks.

"Yes," Jake says. "And don't call me boss."

Someone opens the car door. Jake steps out and the crowd cheers, flashbulbs pop. He smiles down at me and holds out his hand. We walk to the red carpet. The actors pose for photographers.

Behind the posers I see Easton Wolfe absorbed in his phone, scrolling. His brow is furrowed, his face pulled into a frown and yet, he's still so handsome.

I remind myself that I don't give a damn about Easton. I don't care about the way he moves, his shoulders broad, the set of his jaw, firm, the angle clean and sharp.

And it dawns on me that something or is it someone is missing from this picture. Amelia's nowhere to be found. I thought for sure she was going with him to the premiere. I check my phone but there's nothing from her. Maybe she's already inside and he just got here late.

'Not your concern,' Queasy says.

Queasy's right. I'm here for the man who's walking next to me. The handsome sweet man holding my hand. I remember Nikki's advice. I shut my phone down and slip it back in my bag. I smile up at Jake Keller and brush my shoulder against his. "Break a leg."

THE AFTER PARTY'S AT A SMALL WINERY IN MALIBU. THE driver drops us off in front and the crowds part for Jake. Inside, multi-colored balloon lights dangle from wooden rafters. Uniformed waiters circulate with wine and appetizers. Bars and buffet tables are stationed in clusters along the perimeters. A DJ plays Reggae fusion music. You can practically see the endorphins flying like lit sparklers in the air.

People gather around Jake shouting congratulations like he's the second coming . He smiles. It's his night and so far it's a good night and I couldn't be happier for him.

"I'm going to freshen up," I say. "Back in a few."

I'M WALKING OUT OF THE BATHROOM AS PINKIE STEIN'S walking in. "Evie," she says, placing a bejcweled hand on my arm. "Spare me a moment."

She steers me to the party's sidelines. "The movie's been

well-received. Jake's going to get offered meatier parts because of this. He's upping his game, handling all the attention better. I know that Ray Stark gave you a rough time when you first got here, but I just want to say thank you."

"You're welcome," I say. "But I haven't really done anything yet."

"We'll agree to disagree," she says. "You know, one of these days we should have a drink or two. Hop a red-eye to Cabo. We could be sipping Bloody Mary's lying next to an infinity pool overlooking the ocean. I know just the place."

"Sounds perfect," I say, covering a smile.

AN HOUR LATER I'VE CHATTED WITH A THIRD OF THE people here. Now I make small talk with a few investors from Cleveland while Jake mingles. He circles back to me every fifteen minutes or so, and kisses me on the cheek. He seems happy. Ray keeps an eye on him from a few yards away. Pinkie's holding court with a few young actors. She reclines on a couch in the far corner, her feet up on some guy's lap.

Easton divides his time talking to money types and checking his phone. Amelia never showed up and I'm okay with that. But now Easton's been sitting in the same chair for half an hour, glued to his phone. Something's wrong.

I'm having a hard time even looking at him because every time I do I get chills. Something is dark and heavy and just plain wrong. His anger is replaced with sadness. His bravado's shuffled to the side, swapped out by grief. He stuffs his phone in his pocket, and slips onto the patio.

Other than the guys from Cleveland, no one at this party is paying attention to me. I'm not a producer or a studio head. No one's going to pitch me a story. The only person who cares about me here is Jake and he's still running on adrenaline. "It was awesome meeting you," I say to the Cleveland crew. "Have to run."

I edge through the crowd and walk outside. Easton's making his way past the picnic tables, navigating around the attendants clearing up. He pauses at the staircase on the edge of the property, right where the bluff falls into thin air. Framed against the moon sinking low over the Pacific, he opens the gate and walks down the stairs.

"Hold up," I say, but he doesn't hear me over the music. A few wooden steps down I kick off my heels and dangle them from one hand. I head down the stairs, one flight, then the next, until I step onto the sand, a shock of gritty coldness traveling up my legs to my core. I shiver and follow Easton down the beach, skirting random piles of thick seaweed. "Hold up."

He turns. "What are you doing?"

"Clearing my head. Where's Amelia?"

"I told her to go home," he says, and keeps walking.

"Why?" I catch up to him.

The moon's hanging low, yellows, blues and purples shifting across its swollen roundness as it rises above the ocean. The thin beach stretching in front of us is studded with rocks and boulders, lined with jaw-dropping *Conde Nast* cover worthy homes probably cost tens of millions of dollars each.

"You were right," he says. "Amelia wants the dream: the loyal besotted husband, the house in the suburbs, the kids."

"There's nothing wrong with that," I say.

"I agree. But I'm not that guy. I could be selfish and keep her around for longer. Let her develop more feelings for me when I already know I'll never have any for her."

"Why not?" A psychotic push-pull of emotions courses through me. Relief that he let her go ping-pongs with loyalty for my friend.

"Because I just know. Look at you with the determined thrust to your jaw," Easton says, leaning down, rolling his pants up his legs. "You're a warrior, Evie. Do you know that?" He smiles at me for a second.

His smile cracks my heart. Have I ever seen Easton smile?

He resumes walking.

"You told me I was Liam Neeson in every action movie ever," I say and follow.

"That too." He treads the boundary between the surf and the sand, ocean water splashing his muscular calves. "You already pointed out why I shouldn't lead Amelia on. Then the fates intervened, telling me in no uncertain terms that life's too short for bullshit. I gave your pal a big tip, apologized, and sent her home."

"Why'd you come out here?" I ask. "It looked like you were negotiating a business thing."

"I was." He bends down and picks up some small stones that the tide had deposited on the shore.

I wait for one of his mean come backs, but nothing awful pops out of his mouth and that confuses me. "Do you want to tell me what you're thinking about?"

"Not really," he says, tossing a few rocks into the ocean. He continues moving down the beach.

I know with one hundred percent certainty that Easton has hated me ever since I bumped into him at Wyatt's wedding in Vegas a year and a half ago. He made it abundantly clear by 'banning' me from any club, hotel, business, any speck of dust on any street that he owns.

After I got back to Chicago I Googled him, and discovered that Easton Wolfe actually owns quite a lot of specks. "Why don't you tell me anyhow?" I say, hustling to keep up with him.

"Do you know what happened to us after the accident?"

'Buckle up,' Queasy says.

"I heard your family moved to L.A."

"El Segundo," he says. "Right next to some oil fields, close enough to the airport to feel the rattle of the planes as they landed. Not very fancy."

"Not everyone grows up with a silver spoon in their mouth."

"My dad sobered up after the accident, and started dealing with his anger. My parents went to therapy. He and Mom concentrated on Wyatt and me. They turned their lives upside down for us."

"That's great," I say. At least someone's parents got their shit together after the accident. Gossipy sorts speculated something twisted in Easton's brain during the accident. Trauma turned him into a money-making genius. He became a multi-millionaire at the ripe old age of twenty-five. Now, at thirty, he's a billionaire. You'd never know it from looking at him, though.

We walk in silence. He picks up stones, rolls them over in his hands, pitching the ones he doesn't want back into the surf. "Sometimes when I'm confused, I come out to the beach. I pick up stones. I put my fears and my anger into one, or two, or ten," he says. "And then I throw them into the ocean." He flings one into the water. "I don't know why but it makes me feel little bit better."

"You okay?" I ask.

"Not really." He hands me a stone. "Go ahead. Try it."

I concentrate and then hurl the rock into the ocean.

"Good one," he says and hurls another. We walk in silence, the sounds of the party dimming in the background against the rumble of the waves.

Something inside me aches to make things right with Easton. Maybe it's because I can't bring myself to reach out to Wyatt. He's been happily married going on two years now. We haven't talked since the accident thirteen years ago, and

I'm not about to risk breaking our silence. I'm not about to risk breaking Wyatt Wolfe again. Yet when it comes to Easton, this feeling follows me around, nipping at my heels.

'Maybe if you can get Easton to forgive you?' Hope says. *'Maybe you can forgive yourself.'*

I've always wanted the Wolfe brothers' forgiveness. I've prayed about it. I've shed tears over it. I count *three, two, one* and sink into that meditative level within myself. On the outside I look dressed for a party but on the inside I'm frantically stripping.

I peel away boundaries, drop armor, abandon the tools in my arsenal that make me feel safe. I set aside my humor that works like a charm when I need to deflect uncomfortable questions. I leave my quick wit propped up like a sturdy umbrella at the door.

At this very moment my soul is bare, my heart is unguarded and I do what I've longed to do for thirteen years – I supplicate. Easton Wolfe doesn't know it yet but if I had to? If he asked me? I would get down on my knees and beg for his forgiveness. And even though I've wanted to do this for years, I am completely, thoroughly, freaked out.

'Don't do this,' Queasy says. *'Think about the job. Think about Jake Keller.'*

But it's too late. I am too far gone. I don't have a choice.

The gift of forgiveness stands in front of me in the flesh, not wearing a different man's face, not wearing a different man's skin. For the first time I am granted the opportunity to request absolution from someone who can genuinely bequeath it.

And so, I humble myself because forgiveness is more important than looking right. Forgiveness is more important than being right. "Easton," I say. "Do you think we can ever get past the accident? Do you think you can ever forgive me?"

He paces on that hard strip of sand, the ocean waters

splashing across his feet. "Why, after all these years, are you concerned about my forgiveness?" he says.

"I've always wanted to ask for forgiveness. Yours. Wyatt's. Your parents."

"Cross my parents off your list," he says.

The wind off the ocean kicks up and rustles his thick hair. A few errant strands blow about as he picks up more rocks and tosses them. It's all I can do to stop my hand from reaching to smooth them off his face. "Why?"

"They figured the time your mom served was the only resolution they'd ever get. It took them about five years, but when Wyatt graduated high school and made his way down that aisle with a cane instead of a walker, they found acceptance. They moved on."

"Good," I say swallowing hard. "Wyatt?"

"Moved on," he says, walking away from me. "He underwent dozens of surgeries, Evie. Shattered bones. Ripped cartilage. Torn organs. Skin grafts. Brain surgeries. He had to choose between holding onto needing to talk to you, needing to make sense of his feelings, and just dealing with his physical pain. Wyatt was in a lot of pain, you know."

"Right," I say. Hot tears hit the back of my eyes and I struggle to blink them back.

"He was thirteen," Easton says. "His hormones were kicking in, things were starting to change. He had to learn how to talk in full sentences again, learn how to walk again. He got the best surgery, the best physical and occupational therapy. Considering everything, he did great, but there was one lingering problem."

"What?"

"You. He couldn't let go of you."

"Oh," I say, because I left my smart words at the door. I wouldn't know what to say, even if my smart words were gathered as arrows resting in a quiver, itching to be shot in my defense.

"A shrink told Wyatt that sometimes we have to choose between people we love and ourselves. Picking himself meant choosing healing. It took almost a year of counseling, but Wyatt finally separated from you. He chose healing."

"Good," I say, tears welling. I turn, blinking them back, and stumble away from Easton because I do not want him to know. I don't want him to see. Supplication is one issue. Humiliation is another.

It feels weird for all of five seconds to hear that Wyatt let me go. Then it feels like the biggest weight in the world lifts off my shoulders. Heat rises in waves off my skin. The veil of sorrow I have worn for years evaporates. And I finally know, in the marrow of my thin bones, that Wyatt Wolfe has healed from the accident.

I take a breath and almost pass out from the oxygen flooding my brain. This is the first deep, first true breath I have taken in thirteen years. I am intoxicated. I inhale more deeply because this feels like no drug I've ever taken. It's oxygen mixed with freedom and the absence of guilt.

The salt from the ocean air is pungent and my nose crinkles as if I am smelling salt for the first time. I open my eyes and I see clearly for the first time in years because the fucking crown of thorns that was smashed into my head when the Wolfe brothers bounced off our car has been lifted. I stare up at that haunted moon as the ocean waves crash on the beach, and I shiver at the beauty of it all. Either that, or I'm shivering because of the gorgeous man standing in front of me.

The brother of the first boy I fell in love with.

The man who hates me.

Easton Wolfe.

I long to pull him to me. I long to run my hand through

his wild boy hair, feel the thick strands slipping through my fingers. I want to run my thumb over his high cheekbones. I'm consumed with this desperate need to bite his full, wild-boy lips. I need to kiss him. To feel his lips on mine. Feel his tongue slip inside my mouth. Wrap a muscular hand around my waist and pull me to him.

I want to feel his erection growing fast and thick and hard and pressing insistently against my pelvis. I grow wet just thinking about him undoing the buttons on my blouse one by one and running a hand over my lace bra, my nipple pebbling under his touch.

'Easton,' I say.

'Evie,' he says. 'I've wanted you since I saw you in Vegas.'

He slips his fingers inside my bra and palms my breast. He lowers his head and takes it in his mouth. He slides his tongue over my nipple, licking, exploring. He sucks and bites. He flicks my bra open with his other hand and palms my other breast, then plays with the nipple with his thumb and forefinger.

I inhale sharply, my breath leaving my body.

He skims his hand down my chest, down my stomach until he reaches for the zipper on my dress and pulls it open.

But I do not kiss him.

I do not kiss him because that would be a horrible, shitty thing to do to Jake because he is my client, and I like him a lot, and he trusts me and right now — I am his and his alone. Going behind his back would be a betrayal and I don't like to live in betrayal.

I've felt my share of betrayal. I've felt its consequences, and so I do my very best not to do that kind of shit to people. And it dawns on me I'm not really sure who I'd be betraying if I kissed Easton.

Jake Keller who's in that gorgeous winery on the cliff over-looking this beach?

Wyatt Wolfe, the dark floppy haired boy I tried to save thirteen years ago?

Or Dylan McAlister, the man I fell in love with who can't seem to put a ring on my finger?

Suddenly, I am horribly confused.

I need to buy time.

I need to get the hell out of here.

I pull my phone from my purse and turn it back on. "Easton," I say. "I'm so sorry but I need to go back inside. Can we talk about this more later?"

"Sure," he says. "Sure." He continues walking down the beach, walking away from me.

19

72 HOUR HOLD

72 HOUR HOLD

BY THE TIME I GET BACK TO THE HOUSE I FINALLY GET reception and *ping-ping-ping* I am inundated with texts.

> **Ruby:** *Mom had an episode. Call me.*

> **Ruby:** *I'm driving up to the Institute.*

I scroll down, my hands trembling.

> **Ruby:** *Where are you?*

I break out into a sweat.

> **Ruby**: *I know you're working.*

> **Ruby:** *You're always working. Just text me.*

Ruby: Jesus Christ, WTF is wrong with you? This is the emergency we've been worried about. This is the one we've been prepping Plan B for all these years.

Ruby: Did you turn off your fucking phone?

I click Ruby's number and she picks up. "What's going on with Mom?"

"She's alive. Breathing. Conscious. Still here, thank God."

"What happened?" I ask.

"You first," she says. "Where are you?"

"L.A. Tell me what happened?"

"She had another split. The Institute kicked her up to lock down ward for a 72 hour hold."

"She's all right?" I ask.

"What do you define as 'all right?'"

"Just talk to me."

"Where do I begin?" Ruby says. "Mom's not sure where she is. She's asking the nurse if we're still living in that dilapidated house we grew up in with Kyle, her loser boyfriend from before the accident. Something about a bad man coming for her kids if she falls asleep? Is that what you define as 'All right?'"

"No," I say.

"Me either."

There's a long pause.

"Come home, Evie. Come home now." She clicks off.

My world is spinning. I need to get out of here. Now. I need to go home. I glance around but I don't see Jake.

'Get the hell out of Dodge,' Queasy says.

'Just move,' Hope says.

I squeeze past pockets of Hollywood power players chatting each other up. I dodge a waiter holding a tray of appetizers, and bump into another passing in the opposite direction. "I'm sorry," I say.

"No worries," the waiter says.

I keep moving as fast as I can, blow through the front doors and hustle down the sloped driveway, shoving tears away with the heels of my hands. I tell the valet guys I don't have a car, *thank you*, and exit the estate through the front gates.

I walk down Pacific Coast Highway tapping my phone repeatedly to order a ride but I'm in one of those weird, wonky, internet -free spots in Malibu. I can't seem to pull up a ride let alone anything to preserve my sanity. I'm so wound up, that I will walk back to Jake's home if I have to.

Cars zip by me and the rush of the air off them buffets me as I march down the narrow, curvy road that hugs the ocean on one side and cliffs that rise precipitously on the other. I punch the app on my phone repeatedly like a madwoman until – voilà – I get reception.

I order a ride and pace back and forth because I need to burn energy before my hair catches fire. I text Jake and apologize for leaving him high and dry. I tell him something has come up. It's unexpected, important and it's something I have to deal with.

I feel like the world's biggest asshole.

Evie: *I'm sorry, Jake.*

Evie: *So sorry.*

Evie: *I'll get a hold of you in a few days.*

Evie: *I know this is contractual but you are important to me.*

Evie: *I will make this right by you.*

Evie: *I promise.*

Evie: *I'm so sorry.*

A white sedan pulls over with its rideshare light glowing in the dashboard.

I open the back door.

"How's your night?" the driver asks.

"Let's talk about yours," I say.

HALF AN HOUR LATER THE DRIVER DROPS ME OFF AT JAKE'S place. Queen music blares as I walk through the laundry room, then the kitchen, choking on my anxiety. I make my way to the guys and Nikki shooting pool in the adjoining family room. Beer and pizza is scattered around like it's a normal person's house – not Jake Keller's.

"Back so early?" one of the guys asks.

"Yes," I say and keep walking, my head down.

"Evie?" Nikki asks. "Everything okay? Why are you and Jake home so early?"

"Just me," I say. "Don't let me interrupt your game."

Once in my room I burst into tears and sink to my knees, one hand clamped over my heart, the other against my mouth hoping that if I press hard enough maybe I won't scream out loud because Mom broke down again and I am scared out of my mind.

All the money I spent.

All the time I invested.

Every guy I slept with to heal.

Every single damn thing I've done to help Mom isn't working. I have to do what I've always dreaded: leave work before I've finished a job.

I need to hold Mom's hand. I need to look into her eyes and rub her shoulders. We'll figure out this latest bump in the road together just like we always do. I'll buy her a present, tell her funny stories, make her laugh with silly jokes and impersonations of pompous people. Maybe Mom and I will just play out the oh-so-popular mother-daughter frustration game with each other. 'You don't visit me enough,' she'll complain.

'I'm paying your medicals,' I'll counter.

'I'll go without,' she'll say, sticking her chin out defiantly the same way I do when I'm wound up.

'You're going nowhere. You'll stay here and get the best care,' I'll say.

'You don't get to decide that,' she'll retort.

'Yes, mom,' I'll say. 'Actually, I do. Because someone in this family has to be the adult and that falls on me.'

She'll start crying and I'll feel like the world's biggest asshole. I just *love* figuring out thorny, awkward problems with anger – said no one ever. And yet through laughter or sadness or anger we might not always get a happily-ever-after but we reach some kind of temporary fix. We deal. We survive. We live to be a family for another day.

I walk to the closet and pull out my suitcases. I rip my clothes from hangers and pitch them inside the bags. What went wrong with Mom? She was doing so well. Maybe I should have stayed behind? Maybe I should have taken her to that lake house? Maybe this whole thing is my fault.

There's a *knock-knock-knock* on the door. "What?"

"Me," Nikki says.

"Come in."

She enters, juggling two frosty long-necked beer bottles in one hand, holding a box of pizza in the other. "You probably already ate the fancy food at the party. Just in case."

"I seem to have missed the fancy food." I accept a bottle

from her and take a swig. I yank open the armoire and pull out folded tops, bras, and underwear.

"You're leaving?" she asks.

"Yes." I walk into the bathroom, and jam cosmetics, my toothbrush, and shampoo into a toiletry case.

She stands in the doorway. "Why?"

"Emergency back home."

"Does Jake know?"

"I texted him." I pause and look at her, regret eating me up inside. "I feel horrible leaving like this but an emergency came up with my mom."

"You have to go," she says. "I'll drive you to the airport. Do you have a ticket yet?"

"No."

"I'll get you one." She pulls out her phone.

"Thank you," I say, my mind spinning. What if this really is Mom's bad split? The one that puts her back into crazy land for good. What if the past two years she's spent getting her brain zapped and popping new experimental drugs has been for nothing?

I am overwhelmed. I sit down on the floor next to the suitcases and plant my forehead in my hands. "Would you tell Jake I'm sorry? I think he'll hear it coming from you. I think you're the one person here who he genuinely cares about."

"Make that two people."

Jake is standing in the doorway, concern etched on his face.

"I'm sorry," I say still seated as exhaustion bears into my bones. The years of worrying about Mom and Ruby. The years of trying to make everything okay. The years of covering for the fact that my mom can just lose it and we don't know why. It's embarrassing and it's tragic and we love her and she loves us and yet the whole thing is a big mish-mash.

I had hope – real, pinch me, I-can-feel-it hope – for the

last two years that things could heal, and things could be better for Mom. But apparently, I'm just fooling myself because it's looking more and more like things will never be better.

The perfect storm is here. The moment I've been dreading, where real life intrudes on work life. Just like the car aimed at the Wolfe boys thirteen years ago it's on a collision course and it's too late for me to stop it. I feel like an imposter. I'm letting Mom down. I'm letting Jake down. I'm letting Ma Maison down. Considering there's a shuffling of ownership in a few days, I might even be out of a job and letting myself down, too.

'You're being too hard on yourself.' Hope admonishes.

'Disagree,' Queasy says, stumbling about my stomach like a drunk on a bender. *'Smart girls don't take shit for granted.'*

I haven't been able to break through to Jake. I haven't been able to track down his bitter belief that's undermining him.

He walks into the room. Movie stars are supposed to arrogant, egotistical assholes. I never would have called it in a million years that he'd be so sweet, so caring.

"I'm leaving you high and dry and I feel horrible," I say. "I'm not normally the person who promises the world but then abandons any and all on a whim." I swipe a hand through my hair and rack my brain trying to think of the right thing to do, or say, and find a way to make this up to him. "I'll call you when I get back home. We'll figure it out. I promise."

"Of course, we'll figure it out," he says. "I'm coming with you."

20

BROKEN

BROKEN

"No. Stay here. People need you to be here."

"That's the point, Evie. For the most part, they don't. I ask myself every single day why I'm staying here. Why I'm even doing any of this." He takes my hand. "I want to come with you."

His hand is so big and warm. I'm supposed to be the healer and yet he heals me with his kindness. "Why?"

"I know what it feels like when your world is ripped out from underneath you." He looks into my eyes the same way he looked into the eyes of the girl in the movie. Except this is real life and he's not acting and neither am I.

I am just Evie.

He is just Jake.

We are just two people who happened to meet because he is broken and maybe if we're both lucky I can still help him heal.

"When you want to help, and you want to say the right things, or just say anything, but it feels too big and you don't know where to start? I've been there," he says.

He gets it. I relax for the first time since I got the news. I relax since the first time I found a blue box on my bed filled with cut hair. "Okay."

WE TAKE A RED-EYE, AND THE NEXT MORNING I'M BACK AT the Institute outside of Milwaukee. I told Jake the nuts and bolts about the accident on the plane home.

Now, I sit across from Ruby in the dining room on an uncomfortable teal-colored vinyl chair. "Mom was doing well," I say and chew on a ragged fingernail.

"Yeah, things change. What's up with you landing here at the Institute with Jake Keller? Just when I thought I'd seen it all, you throw me another curve ball. How do you even *know* him?"

"He's a client. Tell me more about Mom."

"I got a phone call from the doctor. He said Mom's moods were growing increasingly erratic. He thought something might have triggered her." Ruby uncrosses her long legs. "Remember I told you she was hiding pills? I called but you never picked up."

"You know I turn off my phone when things get busy at work."

"I get that Jake Keller's a big client but you act like every client's a huge deal."

"It's my job, Ruby. It pays the bills."

"With the exception of Jake Keller, corporate consulting's just work. It's not like you're a brain surgeon, flying off to a war in a foreign country to rescue damaged, broken, people."

It's all I can do not to slap her. "I help people."

"You crunch numbers for bigwigs. You assist them with industry trends and forecasts."

"It's a little more than that," I say.

"Get real. Do you even remember what it's like to walk among average people? People who wonder if their credit card is going to be accepted when they buy groceries? Normal people with normal people problems?"

"You're the last person allowed to judge me." I stand up and pace the room. "Isn't Mom always triggered? Isn't that why she's here at the Institute? Isn't that what all the therapy is for? Everyone's trying to find ways to 'un-trigger' her?"

"Yes and no," Ruby says. "I came by to see her a week ago and Mom kept talking about a letter. Some letter was bugging her."

Oh, hell no. My skin prickles, all the little hairs on the back of my arms standing straight up. "What do you mean, *'letter'*? What kind of letter? Did someone say something about me in this letter?"

"I don't know. I didn't read it." She sighs and rolls her eyes. "Besides, it's not always about you, Evie. I asked the people here— the aides, the caretakers. They said Mom's had a few visitors, but no new correspondence. No one's sent her anything in months except for you and me."

"Jesus, Ruby. I pay for your college. I pay for Mom to be here. Medicaid Part B doesn't spring for pudding cups, drugs, group therapy, macramé classes, and brain-zapping magnets. You know what?" I stalk toward the dining room's double doors and throw one open so hard it practically flies off its hinges. "Don't worry about it."

"Where are you going?"

"I'm going to find out what's really going on with Mom because the only time anything gets done in our family is when I step up to the plate. And for the record, Ruby? It's not about me. I wish it were about me. But it's never, ever about me."

I SIT ACROSS FROM MOM IN HER TINY ROOM. SHE'S SO TINY, frail, her salt and pepper hair unkempt, her nails ragged. She looks like hell, dark bags around her eyes from being pumped up on anti-psychotic meds. She sits in a vinyl recliner, deliberately clicking the remote at the TV. I could read all my email by the time she scrolls through three channels.

I reach for the remote. "Let me do that."

"No." She pulls away from me. "I'll do it."

If I had just taken her to that lake house maybe she wouldn't have had this episode. Maybe I let her down. Maybe I fucked things up yet again. How many ways can I fuck things up? How many ways can I break people?

"I've got this," Mom says. "I'll get CNN on this TV if it kills me. Isn't that anchor with the muscular arms and shoulders handsome?"

"Yes." I sigh.

"This is just a temporary setback," she says. "Stop worrying."

"Ruby says you got upset after you read a letter. Do you still have it?"

"I think so, yes."

There's a knock on the door. A woman wearing floral scrubs peeks in. "Maureen?"

"Come in," Mom says, smiling at her.

She takes Mom's vitals. "How are you doing this afternoon?"

"Fine," Mom says. "Better now that my daughters are here to see me."

"Nice. I noticed you have company." She hands Mom a pill and a cup of water. "You know the drill."

Mom drops the pill in her mouth.

"I'm Evie. Thanks for taking such great care of Mom." I look at her nametag. "Dot."

"Absolutely." Dot watches as Mom swallows. "She talks about you. A lot. She said your job was high profile but I still can't get over you showing up here with Jake Keller. Someone talked him into signing autographs in the patient's lounge. He's so down to earth."

"I know, right? Mom said something about a letter," I say. "Can I see it?"

"Up to Maureen," she says, re-filling Mom's water.

"I'm her proxy."

"Evie can see anything," Mom says. "Look. I finally got my channel on the TV."

"Awesome," Ruby says and enters.

Dot pulls open one of the dresser's drawers, and hands me a small plastic bin. "Maureen's correspondence. We don't throw anything away."

I take the container and sort through her mail: birthday cards, Christmas cards, Easter cards, Get Well cards all from Ruby and me. There are also solicitation letters addressed to Mom from charities, and letters from a few from folks whose names sound familiar but I don't really remember them. Then I find an envelope with a name that I do remember.

Kyle Monroe.

We lived with Kyle for nine months when Mom was dating him. She was breaking up with Kyle that cold winter day she had the manic episode. The day we ran over the Wolfe brothers. The day that changed our lives.

The envelope is open, and I pull out the paper, worn and weary around the edges. My heart beats faster, like I'm back on that cold winter day in Wisconsin watching Mom squeeze over-stuffed grocery bags into our beat-up car. My stomach cramps and I break out in a sweat.

'Maybe you shouldn't look at this letter,' Queasy says.

'Maybe Ruby should look at this letter,' Hope says.

But I'm the older sister and I have to be the strong person. I have to be rock for Ruby as well as for Mom. I squeeze my eyes shut and concentrate.

Dear God:

This one scares me. Hold my hand. Walk me through it. And this I ask for in the name of the Father and the Son and the Holy Spirit. Amen.

I cross myself. And then I read.

Dear Maureen:

I hope you don't mind that after all these years I'm writing to you. Don't ask how I tracked you down here. You know I was always good with that kind of stuff.

It's been thirteen years since we spoke. And I finally did what you asked. I went to therapy. I've been counseled by smart people with degrees. They're the experts, not me. They say it's never too late to make amends. That it's good to reach out to those you might have harmed because of your addiction. So, I'm reaching out.

We were living together. You, me, the girls, as a family for almost a year, and then one day out of nowhere you started acting funny. Suspicious. You started asking too many questions, and picked fights. You accused me of sneaking around, of doing horrible things and bam, out of nowhere – you took the girls and left.

I'm shivering, the little hairs on my arms standing straight up and my lips are burning like I accidentally brushed them against hot sauce, the kind Kyle liked with his taco chips when he watched football games.

The accident was awful but you know, Maureen, the Wolfe brothers weren't the only ones hurt that day. The cops tracked your phone records, saw we were texting and questioned me. I was just a guy working in a hardware store doing his best to make a living and provide a home and some money for you and the girls.

And the worst of it was, I had no time to explain to you what happened. No time to explain to you that in spite of all your poking, prodding, and all your questions, *nothing* happened.

I rub the bridge of my nose as bad feelings, horrible feelings, surge inside me. Something is off. Like bugs crawling on my skin. Like an uninvited hand grazing my bare leg.

Don't freak out but I checked up on the girls recently. Ruby's in college. From what I can tell by sitting next to her at lunch in the cafeteria one day, she's still a smart-ass just like when she was six-years old.

But Evelyn. Well. Evelyn's a whole 'nother story. She's grown up to be just as beautiful as I imagined. I follow her on social media. Her posts aren't private. Did you know that?

I even wrote her a few letters, kind of like the one I'm writing you. Like a secret pen-pal. After all these years I didn't think you'd mind.

My hands are shaking.
"Are you okay?" Ruby asks.
"I don't know."

Don't forget, Maureen, I didn't know what it would be like to care for a family. I was ten years younger than you. Practically a kid myself when we took up. Ruby had that mouth on her. Evie was so precocious. I didn't plan on screwing up my lower back at work. I didn't plan on taking the drugs for the pain. You have to remember I wasn't myself.

I looked but never touched, Maureen. You can't fault a guy for that. Besides, that was thirteen years ago. A lot of time has passed. Just because one is tempted doesn't mean one acts on that urge. You're Catholic. You, of all people, should know that temptation is human.

Nausea consumes me.
Nausea *is* me.
I can't feel my hands.
I can't feel my feet.
I sit down on the floor because of the rest of the room

feels unstable, the air precarious, like the walls and ceiling are caving in and will soon suffocate me.

This is my amends, Maureen. I looked but I never touched. I was stronger back then. Life changed and took a turn, and here I am. I hope that whatever they're doing for you in that clinic is helping. I was always fond of you.

My best to you. My best to the girls.

I'm sorry for any and all grief I unintentionally caused you.

Best,

Kyle Monroe

21

PUZZLE PIECES

PUZZLE PIECES

———

'BREATHE,' QUEASY BITES LIKE BILE EATING MY GUT. *'YOU are not a rickety shed.'*

'Breathe,' Hope says. *'You survive the storm that blows through.'*

"Mom?' My hands won't stop shaking. "You never told me why we left the house so suddenly the day of the accident."

"You know why," she says, and aims the remote at the TV again. "Bipolar disorder can work like that. You swing in one direction then the other. I made up my mind to break up with Kyle, there was no changing it. I was done. We were out of there."

"Evie?" A weird look comes over Ruby's face. She rips the letter from my hands.

"That's the only reason?" I ask.

"I'm your mother. I don't need to tell you everything. A mother has reasons."

"Oh fuck." Ruby turns a shade of yellow, drops the letter, and bolts out of the room.

It flutters out of her hand and lands on the linoleum floor with an uninvited whisper, uninvited just like the lips brushing against my face after I already went to bed. *'Shh. Shh, Evie,'* uninvited just like when the covers pulled up to my shoulders were pulled gently down.

And I know.

I finally know why we had to leave so quickly on that cold, mean winter day in a small Midwestern town. We had to leave because — not unlike Adam Bachman and his predator priest —there was a violator in sheep's clothing. We had to leave because the kind of hot sauce Kyle liked with his taco chips when he watched football games and drank too much was burning *my* lips. There was a predator in our house.

I never understood the accident. The puzzle pieces felt so random. Ruby puking as I crawled out the back of the car, the Wolfe brothers broken lying on the hard ground. I stumbled past Easton because something in me needed to find his brother Wyatt. Something in me needed to touch Wyatt and heal him.

I never understood why Mom did something full on crazy like blowing under the candy cane-colored barriers descending on the train tracks. I never really understood why I've been paying for this ever since, busting my ass making amends for all the damage. I'm tired. The holes in my soul grow more ragged every day, like a colony of determined moths eating their way through an old sweater.

Mom sits in that vinyl chair biting her lower lip, and for the first time I see past the damaged, broken woman. I see past the woman I love but walk on tiptoes around because I'm scared I'll do or say the wrong thing and hurt her even more. I see instead a woman who wanted to spare her daughters more pain. A mother who wanted to save her girls. And I am flooded with sorrow. And I am flooded with gratitude.

I kneel next to her and take her hand in mine. I stroke the back of it and press it to my cheek. "Why don't you tell me about that day, Mom? All this time and we've never really talked about it."

She starts crying. "Nothing good happened that day."

"Maybe something good *did* happen that day. Maybe you got Ruby and me out of that house before really awful, horrible things happened."

"I had to listen to what I was feeling," she says. "Something wasn't right. I had to listen."

"Did you save us, Mom?" I ask, my tears flowing unchecked.

"I don't know," she says, twisting her hands in her lap. "I won't ever know for sure. I'm sorry, Evie."

"I'm sorry too," I say, my heart cracking because I'm finally putting these puzzle pieces together. All the men I've been working so hard to heal is really about healing Mom. I wrap my arms around her thin shoulders and hug her. "I'm sorry too."

22

LAKE LODGE

CEDAR LODGE

Nikki booked a suite for Jake and me at Cedar Lodge on Lake Wisconsin a few towns over.

Considering the countless times I've visited Mom at the Institute, I've never stayed at this resort and I've always wanted to. I just didn't plan on doing this at the end of "rockets' red glare and bombs bursting through the air" kind of day.

Nikki has taken care of everything. She's already checked us in. I'm still shaky and I'm grateful I don't have to think about details. I clue Jake in on the basics of what happened during my visit with Mom on the drive over. He's kind and respectful. He doesn't push.

The lodge is comforting, the perfect place to be. It's upscale without being pretentious, its wood floors heavy and dark, covered with thick tapestry area rugs in rich colors.

Floor to ceiling windows look out over a gorgeous lake, the boats tucked safely into slips.

We check into our private cabin, shower, then make our way back to the lodge. Jake grabs us beer and sandwiches from the bar, and we walk down to the dock. We sit on the edge, roll up our jeans and dangle our feet into the lake below.

"I'm giving Kyle's letter to the cops along with the ones I got in L.A.," I say, picking at my sandwich.

"Good," he says."Do you think Kyle's the person writing your letters?"

"I don't know." I shrug. "I'll let police figure it out."

"You going to be okay?" He drapes an arm around my shoulders.

"Yeah," I say, leaning back against his chest. The place is quiet. There's not many people here this weekday late afternoon. The trees rimming the lake houses are still leafy green, the air fresh and clean. The shimmer of the sun dropping lower over the water warms my face. I inhale and wonder if this is how life's supposed to feel – relaxed, sweet, comforting – until a mosquito lands on my arm. I jump and slap it. "Ow!"

"The obligatory asshole showing up at the perfect party." Jake says.

"I was supposed to vacation at a lake house before I accepted the gig to work with you," I say. "My boss told me the mosquitoes would eat me alive. I laughed at her."

"Don't you hate when those people are right? Are you happy you made that choice? Are you glad you came to L.A.?"

"Yes," I say and take a swig of my beer. "You?"

"Absolutely. I think I'm back on track."

"I think so too. You were shut down, Jake. Everyone gets wounded. But sometimes we get triggered and a wound festers," I say. "Then we struggle with the ugliness. We fight it, drown it in booze, medicate it, or we just shut down. "

"Enough about me, he says. "The last two days have been super rough for you. How do you feel?"

"In a weird way, relieved," I say, tipping back my beer. "Like I was finally given a clue to a mystery that was never solved — until now. And now life can be different. Now I can move on."

And I realize — there are no accidents. Jake and I came together for a reason. I can find a way to move forward — maybe Jake can too. "Remember when you said that you left the church in high school?"

"Yes," he says.

"Adam told me about Father Tate. Did you see Father Tate do something bad to Adam?"

"That's so long ago," he says. "Let's not talk about that. Maybe when your Mom is feeling better you should come back to L.A."

I'm going to miss Jake Keller. I'm going to miss him for a long time.

I stand up and brush the dust from the wooden dock off my pants. I look out over the gorgeous lake, and picture casting a line out, feeling the tug of a fish's bite when it takes the bait. I picture myself reeling it in and pan-frying it on a grill while hanging out with my friends and my family and Jake Keller or Dylan McAlister on a dock like this.

I hold out my hand to Jake. "Come on. We've got work to do."

———

I stare into Jake's face as he fucks me. My legs are wrapped over his shoulders. His cock is buried deep inside me. He's skirting that border between the earthly plane and the ecstasy of a mind-bending orgasm.

I bite my lip and exhale his name. "Jake."

"What?" He thrusts into me harder.

I know where the poison exists in Jake's body. It's in his throat. It's in his chest. "Do something for me?"

"Anything," he says and turns me on my side, pressing one knee toward my chest. He grabs a pillow, and presses it under my knee.

"Tell me about the priest from your parish in Albuquerque. Tell me about Father Tate."

"I'm not talking about him now." He grabs my shoulder with, his grip rougher than normal, and sinks back inside me with a fierceness.

I wince. "Tell me what Father Tate said to you that day. The day you caught him hurting Adam."

He penetrates me more deeply, my ass slapping against his pelvis. I squeeze my eyes shut knowing that sometimes the sweetest, kindest people have the roughest time letting go of a wound that has cut them deeply.

"Jake."

"What?"

"Tell me what Father Tate said to you that day."

He grunts, ignoring my request. Instead, he hooks his hands around my pelvis, hoists my ass in the air and fucks me from behind. His cock is deep inside me. "I don't have to talk about this," he says. "I don't have to do anything I don't want to do."

"I know." I grit my teeth because what we're doing right now isn't about sex. This is about his wound hanging onto him with for dear life. This is about lies, and power, deception, abuse. This is about predators taking advantage of those they perceive to be weak.

He rakes his fingers through my hair and goosebumps erupt on the backs of my arms. My nipples harden. My sex clenches from arousal, but this isn't the time to be distracted.

I survived punch-your-throat-out childhood trauma. I

survived abuse and craziness. I might have been a weak and scared little girl before but I'm a 21ˢᵗ century courtesan now. I'll be god damned if the bitter belief that's brought Jake Keller to his knees will be walking on two legs once I'm done with it.

"Jake," I say, fighting back tears. "Tell me what Father Tate said when you caught him with Adam. Just do what I'm asking. *Please.*"

"Father Tate said I could never tell," Jake says. "He said I could never tell because no one would believe me and God would hate me for being a liar."

He stops.

He just stops and I hear him breathing heavily. "Oh."

The taint, the bitter belief, the poison is pouring out of him. It's pouring into this bed, staining it with sorrow. So similar to the poison that leaked drip by drip into that small house Mom and Ruby and I shared with Kyle Monroe and threatened to drown us before we even realized those waters were dangerous. It was why Mom knew she had to get me and Ruby out. It was why we left in such a manic hurry the day we ran over the Wolfe brothers.

"On your back," I say to Jake, trying to catch my breath. "Trust me."

He pulls out of me, turns, and lies on his back, his breath thick and heavy and yet something has already shifted within him. The lie is revealed.

I straddle him. I circle his erection – still hard – with my fist, and stroke it. I rub him against my warm, wet center, and lower myself onto him.

"Oh," he says, biting his lip.

I lower myself onto him as deep as I can go and I fuck him.

I close my eyes and concentrate because I can feel his bitter belief trying to sneak away and hide again and I will not allow that. I fuck him harder until I feel him shudder within me as he comes.

"Evie," he exclaims.

I open my eyes, and stare into his. I lean down and kiss him tenderly. I push back the hair on his forehead clinging to the perspiration on his brow. I place a hand on his throat. "Say it. Tell me. Tell the world what Father Tate said you couldn't."

"I don't know," he says.

"Say it. Get his poison out of you."

I am pulling this cord of lies and deception out of his body. It is thick in his throat. All these congested, confused words queued up like planes waiting to taxi down the runway. "Trust me."

"I saw Father Tate with Adam," Jake says. "I saw him doing things Adam didn't want him to do."

"More," I say, moving my palm to his chest, feeling the roots of the poison entrenched in his heart. I envision pulling those roots out. My palm burns. "There is more. Tell me more."

"Father Tate touched Adam. Father Tate made Adam do things."

"More," I say. This wound is old and mean and ugly but it comes out with a clunk into my hand. I stare at the predator as it wriggles about, as it takes its last thieving, pathetic breaths.

"I told him not to touch me," Jake says. "But Father Tate said no one would believe me. And so he did it anyhow."

"Oh, sweetheart," I say, my heart breaking for my lovely, sweet Jake. "I'm so sorry." I release that negative energy into the Universe so it can be repurposed into something neutral or even positive. Something like kindness, truth, beauty, love.

I wrap my arms around Jake and I hold him, cradle him, caress him, love him. "Your words have power. Your words have meaning. You are taken seriously. Never again, Jake. From here on out you say the words you need to say. You say the important words. Never again."

"Never again."

"NEVER AGAIN," I SAY WHEN WE KISS AT THE AIRPORT IN Milwaukee before he leaves on his flight back to L.A., "will you keep your truth quiet."

"Never again," he says and kisses my hand and then kisses me on the lips. "You're amazing, Evie. Thank you. I'll call you when I'm back in L.A."

"Yes," I say, knowing that he never will. Our work is done. I'm okay with that. "Hey, hot Movie Star."

He swivels and faces me, while people around us take pictures of him.

"I adore you. Break a leg."

"Will do." He hits me with that panty-melting Jake Keller smile, then steps onto the jet way, out of my sight, and out of my life.

23

TORNADOES

TORNADOES

VICTORIA COMES WITH ME WHEN I GIVE MOM'S LETTER TO the detectives. Storm clouds are rolling in over the Chicago skies as we walk ten blocks to our fave beer and burger joint for lunch.

Ping-ping-ping my phone chimes. I'm expecting Dylan. He's arriving tonight and I can't wait to see him.

Ruby: *Mom's back in her old room.*

Evie: *Good.*

Ruby: *They put her in a different room and she said it smelled like cheap perfume.*

Ruby: *She pitched a fit.*

Evie: Which means she's getting better.

Evie: Right?

                                        Ruby: Nailed it.

                                        Ruby: I'm dating a new guy.

Evie: Great!

"Come on," Victoria says. "It's starting to rain."
I pick up the pace.

Evie: Talk more IRT later. Right?

                            Ruby: Mom would like it if you visited her soon.

Evie: Absolutely.

AT THE RESTAURANT WE ORDER SODAS, ICE TEA, A ROUND of sliders and cheesy fries. Amelia joins us and we sit around the high top table, an afternoon Cubs baseball game plastered on at least five TVs mounted on the walls.

"What do you do now?" Amelia asks, dipping into a plate of nachos. "What's the next step?"

"The cops will investigate the Kyle Monroe thing," I say. "They'll track him down."

"They'll figure out if he was the one doing the breaking and entering," Victoria says.

"It sounds like it was him," Amelia says. "But I still can't shake the feeling one of your clients has a hand in this."

"Why?" Victoria asks.

"I get a hunch." She shrugs. "Something I can't quite put my finger on."

"All those years I blamed Mom for everything," I say. "She was taking care of all of us by blowing out of Kyle's place that day."

"Not trying to be a downer," Amelia says, "but she still hit the Wolfe boys."

"I know. Which is tragic, broke my heart, and so many other people's. But after thirteen years I finally get to add another piece to that story. A piece that spells redemption."

"Easton talked about it, you know," Amelia says. "When I stayed with him in L.A."

"I didn't know that."

Queasy flips over and I silently will him to hold his tongue for a change.

"One night Easton sent the chef and the maid home early. He grilled steaks and vegetables, picked a nice bottle of wine, and gave me this bracelet." Amelia points to the diamond jewelry on her wrist.

"Pretty," Victoria says.

"Gorgeous," I say.

"After he cracked open the second bottle of wine he told me about the accident. I knew it was brutal but hearing it from his perspective gave me a whole new appreciation for what went down the day."

"It was brutal," I say. "Nothing will change that."

"I asked him if he had found healing. You know, let go, let God, that kind of thing?"

"What did he say?" I ask.

'Maybe he did let it go,' Queasy says.

'Maybe he doesn't need your forgiveness because he's over it,' Hope says.

"He said it changed his life forever." She tears a packet of sweetener open and stirs it into her iced tea. "I'm not supposed to tell you the rest. He told me not to tell anyone."

"You can't bait us like that," Victoria says.

"Fine, just don't tell anyone."

"Who am I going to tell?" Victoria asks.

"He said if it wasn't for Wyatt he'd be just fine. But Wyatt is fucked up permanently. Wyatt might look almost okay on the outside but he'll always be a mess."

My heart drops so fast it plummets past my feet and shatters on the concrete floor. I stare at my watch in an attempt to cover my feelings. "We should get going."

"We're supposed to be at Ma Maison for a change of management meeting at 4," Victoria says.

"Easton said it marked him forever," Amelia says. "He'll never forget. He'll never forgive."

Something rips open inside me and I cringe. I'll never be able to make this right with Easton Wolfe. He's never going to forgive me.

WE WALK INTO THE MODERN, GLASS ENCASED MID-RISE ON Michigan Avenue that houses Ma Maison. Eight more of Ma Maison's high-end escorts are already gathered in the lobby.

Lily and Scarlett are talking to each other at the far end of the vestibule. Scarlett waves to me.

Amelia punches the elevator button.

My phone starts pinging.

Dylan: *Plane delayed in Louisville. Tornadoes.*

Evie: *Crap.*

Dylan: *I don't know when we're landing. Don't wait up for me.*

Dylan: Miss you.

Evie: *Miss you back.*

And I do. Dylan's my rock. Not the kind I want to throw into the ocean.

Dylan*: Got a surprise for you.*

Evie: *Not holding my breath.*

Dylan: *Good. 'Cause I like my girl with color in her cheeks.*

Dylan*: Love you.*

Evie*: Who are you and where have you hidden my boyfriend, Dylan McAlister?*

Dylan: *Ha.*

Dylan*: See you soon. I've got a key. I'll let myself in.*

Huh? Am I losing my mind? Or am I not remembering stuff?

Evie: *When did I give you a key?*

Dylan*: A few trips ago.*

The elevator door opens. Amelia and Victoria step inside. Five more women join them. Amelia holds the door open for me with her hand, her diamond bracelet glittering. "Come on."

"Don't want to be late," Victoria says.

Dylan: Why? Do you want it back?

Evie: No, dork.

Evie: I def want you to have a key.

Evie: Got to go. Can't wait to see you!

WE STAND IN THE ELEVATOR, APPLY LIPSTICK AND RUN OUR hands through our hair.

"I hope we don't have to re-negotiate our contracts," Amelia says.

"Who's going to be at this meeting?" I ask.

"The new owner," Victoria says. "I practically had to beat that information out of Madame, the tight-lipped bitch, when I landed back in Chicago a week ago," Victoria says. "Thank me later."

"You got her high, didn't you?" I ask.

"Go to hell, Kindergarten." Victoria bursts out laughing. "You know all my tricks."

"That's what you think." I smile at her.

MADAME'S ASSISTANT, JAY, ESCORTS US INTO HER OFFICE. "Thanks," I say.

"Can I get you ladies anything?" He asks.

"No, thank you," I say.

"I'm good," Victoria says.

"We're perfect," Amelia says. "Thank you."

"Madame will be with you shortly," he says and leaves the room.

I walk to the windows and gaze out at the storm clouds barreling across Chicago's skyline and Lake Michigan in all her choppy, white-capped glory.

"Ladies," Madame says, entering. She takes a seat behind her Louis XIV desk all shiny and glossy. "Thanks for coming."

"So excited," one girl says.

"You should be," Madame says. "We've got some exciting news for Ma Maison. New ownership. We're expanding into a few different cities. We're adding and modifying tiers for our independent contractors."

"Independent contractors meaning us?" Scarlett asks.

"Yes. We're adding health care options, incentivizing programs, bonuses."

"Wow," another pretty girl says.

'Something doesn't feel right,' Hope says.

'Get the hell out of Dodge.' Queasy paces.

Madame hits the intercom button on her phone. "Jay. Show in our new CEO, please."

Amelia, Victoria and I look at each other in silent partnership as the door opens.

And in walks Easton Wolfe.

"Madame Marchand. Ladies. I'm Easton Wolfe. Pleased to make your acquaintance. Some of you I've had the pleasure of meeting. Some I haven't."

A buzz builds around the room.

"Yay," Amelia says breaking out in a grin.

"Crap," Victoria mumbles.

I turn and stare out the window. Thunder rumbles, a lightning bolt zaps down from the heavens and strikes in the distance.

I am damned.

I am doomed.

I am exquisitely fucked.

24

YOUR DEVOTED FAN

YOUR DEVOTED FAN

Dear Evelyn:

Sorry I haven't written lately. There's so much going on. Work. Family. You know the drill. It's never ending. Just when I think I've finally got a handle on everything, one leg of the four-legged stool collapses. I'm wobbling around, trying to hold up all the shit, balancing career and life and love. I don't want to drop it all. I don't want all the parts of the game to smash onto the ground and shatter into a million pieces.

It gets so messy when that happens.

You know the blue box I left on your bed? I bought another one recently. Just like yours, but bigger. I keep things in it that remind me of you.

A small bottle of the perfume you wear. A selection of photos of you from over the years. One of your lipsticks. Locks of your hair that your boyfriend, Dylan, cut a few years back. When he was worried about 'bad guys' targeting you. For a smart guy he can be a bit simplistic at times. Almost childlike. I found that in the envelope in your desk drawer. Oh, and I keep a copy of the newspaper article about the day your mom ran over the Wolfe brothers.

You probably think I just pen these letters and send them off as fast as I write them. But I don't. This is hard work for me. Putting words together isn't really my strength. That said, I am pouring my heart out to you on these pages, practically bleeding onto these pages. And yet, no matter how many times I write to you, no matter how many times I give you suggestions on ways to improve your life, you don't change anything.

You keep living your life exactly how you want with no regard or care or kindness for anyone around you. Someday you're going to wake up and realize that the choices you make have consequences. Someday you're going to learn that every action has an equal and opposite reaction. Someday you're going to change your mind.

So here I am trying to figure out a way to move forward. It's not easy. It's a lot of work. I can't survive on hopes and dreams, you know. And much as I love spending my time sending you letters I think I'm going to keep this one to myself – for now.

I'm going to place this 'love letter' in the box with the other ones I haven't sent. How many are there now? Ten? Twenty? I'll put the cover back on, secure it with ribbon, and tuck it away for safe keeping.

I only want what's best for you, Evelyn.

Until next time.

I am, as always,

Your Devoted Fan

DEAR READER: THANKS SO MUCH FOR reading MOVIE STAR. I love writing this series. I hope you enjoyed. If you did, please consider leaving a review on the site where you purchased the book.

Evie's journey continues in BELOVED #3 . Easton Wolfe's taking over ownership of Ma Maison Agency. Dylan McAlister wants to take his relationship with Evie to the next level. Wyatt Wolfe is taking her heart.

But it's Evie's 'Devoted Fan' who wants to take her life...

21st CENTURY COURTESAN is a **sexy, dark, addictive** series filled with love, lust, family loyalty, deceit, revenge, and all the *sweet little things in life worth killing for...* 1-click BELOVED #3.

SIGN UP FOR MY NEWSLETTER TO LEARN ABOUT NEW books and bookish developments.

If you love steamy, angsty, and funny royal romantic comedy that's been described as "... Ms. Congeniality meets Sex and the City..." check out the first book in THE CROWN AFFAIR series The Prince's Playbook #1.

IF YOU ENJOY **TIME TRAVEL ROMANCE** THAT'S SWOONY and packed with thrills — you'll get swept up in The Believer: Jack & Clara - a STAND ALONE in the Mortal Beloved world.

Sign up for my NEWSLETTER and enjoy breaking news about books and special offers.

I'd love for you to join my readers' group at **Pamela DuMond's Dirty Darlings.** Turn the page to read an excerpt of The Beloved. Happy reading.

Xoxo,

Pam

EXCERPT: THE BELOVED

Chapter 2

A LOVER LOST

Present day

I EXIT THE ELEVATOR OF THE ONE MAG MILE HIGH-RISE and stride through the lobby as fast and furious as any car-jacking movie.

I normally say hi to the concierge seated behind the desk in the center of the foyer, but today I ghost him with every click of my thousand dollar Louboutin pumps because he is a kind man. The last thing I want to do to a kind man is spew anger on him because I'm melting down over a not-so-kind man.

Victoria and Amelia follow behind me.

"Slow down," Victoria says, kicking it up a notch, her long, toned legs hustling under her designer skirt.

"I can't." I grind my teeth. "I'm getting the hell out of here."

"Stop," Amelia says. "Just stop for a second and breathe."

"Breathing won't fix this." I roll my neck waiting for my friends to catch up with me. Lightning strikes and thunder rattles the frosted floor-to-ceiling windows. An eerie yellow green mist hangs thick in the Chicago air, the weather as panicked as I feel.

"Better," Amelia says, touching my arm. "How bad can this be?"

"The guy who hates me more than anyone else in the world is our new boss. Easton Wolfe calls the shots at work now." I shrug her off. "You tell me."

"It's awkward and it sucks." Amelia peers out the windows. "But you'll adjust. We survive. That's what we do."

"Change can be good, Evie," Victoria says. "Blow out old energy. Invite in fresh. Like this storm."

"This storm's ushering in a tornado that will kill us all. Besides, Amelia's just happy about Easton Wolfe buying Ma Maison because she likes him."

"When is liking a hot, wealthy man a sin?" Amelia asks.

"Now." I push a door open and step onto the sidewalk seconds before the heavens crack open, pelting us in fat, bloated drops.

"Crap." Amelia puts up a hand to shield her face.

Rain slams down in sheets drenching us.

"This rain is nuts." Victoria throws her purse on top of her head and hails a cab. A taxi veers to the side of Michigan Avenue its tail-lights blinking yellow against the soggy gray and she bolts toward it.

"I'm with her," Amelia says, racing after Victoria.

I hesitate, torn between following them and ducking back inside One Mag Mile. I'm tempted to take an elevator to the basement, stake out a dark corner, hunker down and hide for a week. Discussing the buy-out over drinks and hors d'oeu-vres with my friends won't make my feelings go away. There's too much crazy swirling around.

"Kindergarten," Victoria hollers, standing next to the cab. She calls me by my nick-name, breaking through my stupid wall of stupider thoughts.

I raise a hand to my shield my face, peering at her through the torrential downpour.

"Hurry up." She plunges into the back of the taxi.

I glance at One Mag Mile, then watch Amelia follow Victoria inside the cab. Normally this would be the point that I'd send up a prayer to the heavens for help and guidance. But I'll bet the house Jesus already knows I am exquisitely, excru-ciatingly fucked.

The guy who bought out Ma Maison Agency is Easton Wolfe, the brother of the first boy I fell in love with thirteen years ago. The billionaire genius with the eight-inch scar running from his hip to his thigh; the very scar I helped carve into him when my mom and I ran him over in our car.

I traveled to L.A. recently to help Jake Keller, mega movie star, heal. I stumbled upon Easton at a Hollywood event and tried my best to apologize. I would have done almost anything to earn his forgiveness but forgiveness was not mine to earn.

Maybe I didn't ask Easton the right way. Maybe I didn't pick the right words. Maybe forgiveness slipped away like a lover lost because he didn't accept my apology. Because how do you forgive the person who ruined your biggest childhood dream? How do you forgive the person who mangled you and your brother in a spectacular two for the price of one deal?

I felt horrible, but I understood. The world doesn't revolve around me. Bigger, indecipherable, karmic issues are at play and only God knows what else the Universe has in store for us. Yet, I can't stop asking myself why Easton Wolfe bought out Ma Maison. Perhaps the better question is why do I care?

"I'm melting." Amelia slams the cab door, then quickly kicks it back open. "Stop being an indecisive bitch, Evelyn. Come on."

I give up trying to fight the weather, let alone my feelings, and make my way toward the cab. A little snow didn't kill me thirteen years ago when we ran over the Wolfe brothers. A little rain isn't going to kill me now. I am not weather averse. I am bullshit averse.

Another thunderclap rips with a bang loud enough that pedestrians duck. It's late summer but there's more than a twinge of bittersweet chill in this almost autumn downpour. Out of nowhere a firm hand grips my arm, spinning me around. It's the devil himself.

"I need to talk to you," Easton says, staring down at me with hazel golden eyes.

"No, you don't."

"Yes. Yes, I do."

I rip my gaze from his and stare down at his muscular hand. His grip's firm and yet his knuckles do not blanch because unlike me he's controlled. He knows exactly what he's doing and I shiver. "Fine. Let's set a time."

"Now works for me."

"Now's not going to fly," I say. "I've got plans."

"Change them."

"Just because I'm working for you doesn't mean —"

"Please change them," he says, his voice softening. "Please."

He no longer sounds like a demanding new boss ordering around a subservient employee. He sounds like the boy I used to know before the accident.

"Fine," I say. "Let go of me."

But he doesn't and I can't shake the feeling things

between us are going to get worse before they get better. "*Please* let go of me. It's not like I'm going to run away."

"Evie," Victoria hollers. She arches a brow and worries her lower lip.

Easton releases me and my skin instantly misses the press of his firm flesh.

I wave goodbye to Victoria. "Go."

She holds a hand up to her face in the universal expression for 'Call me.'

Amelia pokes her smiling face out the cab's window and waves. "Easton."

Of course Amelia's cheery. She slept with him a few weeks ago and he gave her a diamond tennis bracelet worth at least 10 K. She'd love a second bite at the hot billionaire, maybe score a matching necklace, or something even bigger — a house in the suburbs bought in cash, with a gardener thrown in for good luck.

"You and Evie should come with us," Amelia says. "We'll play catch up."

"We'll catch up later," Easton says.

"Promise?" She bats her eyelashes.

"Yes," he says. "Of course."

"Okay, boss."

The cab edges away from the curb into screechy, sloppy, stop and go Chicago traffic.

"What do you want to talk about? What's this important thing that can't wait?"

"Where are you going?" he asks.

The rain's relentless. But unlike me, Easton doesn't look like a drowned rat. He just looks slippery and hard and wet. His thick blonde hair is slicked back off his forehead a few lucky drops cling to the feathery tips of his sooty brown lashes.

If I didn't already have a boyfriend I'd be attracted to him.

"Home," I say and bite the inside of my cheek. "I'm going home."

"I'll give you a ride." He places that damn hand back on my arm, his touch gentler this time, and uninvited heat bubbles in my core.

"You say that to all the girls," I protest, but allow him to guide me forward.

"Actually, I don't." He drops his hand to my waist and directs me to a limo, parked in One Mag Mile's loading zone, lights blinking. A driver steps out and opens the passenger door. "By the way," Easton says, "thanks for giving me crap straight out the gate. I expected nothing less from you."

"What are you talking about?"

"The Ma Maison meeting. You demanded I send group health insurance plans to all independent contractors within the week."

"Health care's important." I don't remember a word of what I said twenty minutes ago in that meeting. "Thanks for pointing out that I'm predictable." I slide into the far side of the back seat.

"It's the least I could do." He squeezes in after me. "Michigan and Huron, please," he instructs the driver.

"I don't live at Michigan and Huron."

"I know that." He pushes his damp hair off his forehead.

"Then what are you —"

He places one finger to my lips. "Shh."

I stare up at him not sure what to say, not sure what to feel, not sure where I live anymore.

"I've got a proposal I want to run past you," he says.

"Like a work thing?" I ask, my heart jerking about in my chest. "Like a date? I'm busy this week. My boyfriend's coming into town."

"Not for me, Evelyn." He rolls his eyes like a teenager. "Don't worry about me. I'll never ask you for a date."

"Thank God." His eye roll thing pisses me off. "Saves us that awkward moment of me turning you down. Why don't you tell me your proposal on the way home? I need time to clean my place..."

But he's already turned away, slipping in earbuds, staring out the window. The car's wiper blades beat anxiously across the windshield. I squeeze the fleshy web between my thumb and forefinger hoping the dull pain will relieve some of my own anxiety. I try to read Easton but his face has turned to stone, and I wonder what I'm getting myself into.

BOOKS BY PAMELA DUMOND

THRILLERS

21st CENTURY COURTESAN

Psychological Thriller series (Steamy)

THE PLAYER #1

THE MOVIE STAR #2

THE BELOVED #3

THE HUSBAND #4

THE DEVOTED FAN #5

MORTAL BELOVED

Historical Fantasy Time Travel series (PG-13)

The Messenger #1

The Assassin #2

The Seeker #3

The Believer: Jack & Clara - STAND ALONE

COZY MYSTERIES

ANNIE GRACELAND COZY MYSTERIES

Stand Alones

Cupcakes, Pies, & Hometown Guys

Cupcakes, Paws, & Bad Santa Claus

Cupcakes, Diaries, & Rotten Inquiries

Cupcakes, Sales, & Cocktails

Cupcakes, Bats, & Scaredy Cats

Cupcakes, Bars, & Rock Stars

Cupcakes, Lies, & Dead Guys

Cupcakes, Spies, & Despicable Guys

The Annie Graceland Mystery Set: Books 1 - 4

The Annie Graceland Mystery Set #2: Books 5 - 7

VON PUMPERNICKLE COZY MYSTERIES

GOLDMITTEN: Cozy Animal Mystery #1

<u>'SWEETER' ROMANCE</u>

ROYALLY WED

Romantic Comedy series (PG-13)

Part-time Princess #1

Royally Wed #2

Part-time Poser #3

Royally Knocked Up #4

Royally Wed Box Set: Books 1 - 4

PLAYING SWEETER

Romantic Comedy Stand Alones (PG-13)

Ms. Match Meets a Millionaire

The Story of You and Me

'HOT' ROMANCE

THE CROWN AFFAIR

Romantic Comedy series (Steamy)

The Prince's Playbook #1

His Majesty's Measure #2

The American Princess #3

The Duchess's Decision #4

The Crown Affair Collection: Books 1 - 4

PLAYING DIRTY

Romantic Comedy Stand Alones (Steamy)

The Client

The Matchmaker

The Bodyguard

A Playing Dirty Duet

BOOKS in the WORKS

Dr. Strangedove: Von Pumpernickel Cozy Animal Mystery

For more details please visit Pamela DuMond Author.

ABOUT THE AUTHOR

Pamela DuMond is the *USA Today* Bestselling author of *Part-time Princess* © 2014 and other modern fairytales. Pam writes her own books. #Iwritemyownbooks

Pam writes witty, swoony rom-coms and cozy mysteries. She balances the giggles with darker reads: historical fantasy and psychological thrillers.

Pam's books have been optioned for Film/TV, licensed by Chapters Interactive Stories as games, and featured in *Glamour UK*.

A Midwestern girl at heart, Pam landed in L.A. where on occasion she sticks her toes in the ocean, consumes audio books, and asks 'What do you want now?' to her two funny cats.

————

Sign up for Pam's Newsletter .

Like Pamela DuMond Author on Facebook.

Join Pam's reader group at Pamela DuMond's Dirty Darlings .

Follow Pamela DuMond on Bookbub for timely deals.

Stalk Pamela DuMond on Instagram .

For more information...
www.pameladumond.com

ACKNOWLEDGMENTS

Thanks to to Kelly Hartog for editing. Thanks Lori Jackson for the gorgeous graphics. Thanks Amber Hamilton, PA for handling so many bookish tasks! Thanks Colleen and Itsy Bitsy Bloggers, Caitlyn O'Leary, Maggie Marr, Sylvie Fox, Cindy Sample, Carolyn Haines, Christine Ashworth, Samantha Beck, and "Pamela DuMond's Dirty Darlings" for being such awesome cheerleaders.

Thanks to my readers and supporters Jeanie Whitmire Jackson, Carrie Hartney, D.C., Cheryl Cavitt Carlson, Joan Brady, Christine Ashworth, Beverly Diehl, Maria Seager, Joe Wilson, Kristin Warren, Monica Mason, Nic Conway, Melissa Black Ford, and Rita Kempley, to name a few.

Thank you romance bloggers — you are the best. And a huge thanks to all you readers. You rock!

Xo,

Pamela DuMond